TFF-X

Ten years of *The Future Fire*
A Speculative Fiction Anthology

edited by

Djibril al-Ayad
Cécile Matthey
Valeria Vitale

Futurefire.net Publishing

Contents

Acknowledgements

This celebration anthology would not exist without the generous support of many people who contributed to our fundraiser on IndieGogo, pre-ordered the book or donated money to the campaign; participated in our blog carnival or otherwise helped to spread the word, or donated gifts, rewards and prizes. In particular we should acknowledge our eternal gratitude to Eric Asaris, Belinda Draper, Ernest Hogan, Robin E. Kaplan, Stephanie Saulter, Jared Shurin, Alasdair Stuart and Jo Thomas. The rest of you are far too numerous to mention, but you know who you are!

Preface
Djibril al-Ayad

This anthology celebrates ten years of *The Future Fire* magazine (**futurefire.net**), by both reprinting a few highlight stories from the first thirty-one issues, and including several new, experimental, unusual or aspirational pieces to give a taster of what we'd like to see more of in the next decade.

Issue #1 appeared in January 2005, after a bit of preamble and experimentation the previous year, and apart from a short hiatus to rest up and take stock about halfway through, we've been publishing an average of three to four issues per year ever since. We always wanted *TFF* to be challenging, experimental, progressive, inclusive, political, revolutionary—even if to start with maybe we weren't sure what we were rebelling against!

The first thing you would notice if you went back in time ten years (or just used the Internet Archive's Wayback Machine) to look at the *TFF* website in 2005, would be how god-awful-shitty the web design was. I like to think that's aesthetics having changed, and it wasn't quite so '90s-looking to a 2005 eye, but I'm lying to myself. Still, the evolution from CBBC-quality flames in 2005, via a slightly darker, smoky aesthetic in 2007, to the cathode ray tube Unicode-soup we know and love today in about 2009, echoes the growing confidence we started to have in our niche in the speculative fiction market.

We launched in 2005 as a cyberpunk market (words like "chrome," "postmodern" and "hyperfiction" peppered our tagline, manifesto and first story contests), but through an accident of community we knew more writers of horror and dark fantasy, and there was almost no conventional scifi in the first several issues. You can hear a bit of diffidence about this in our early editorials, and our craving for that elusive cyberpunk is almost tangible...

But once our slushpile was deep enough that we could reasonably select on genre and theme as well as quality (we were *always* uncompromising on quality) then our niche was under our control, and we didn't have to be shy about the geeky, retro, techno-noir look we imagined for ourselves. Not that we ever stopped publishing horror, fantasy and surreal stories as well, of course; and never will.

You might also notice the evolution in our one-line mission statement: "New writing in Dark Speculative Fantasy!" we proclaimed in 2004. "Speculative Fiction, Cyberpunk and Dark Fantasy!" we boomed in 2007. "Social-Political and Speculative Cyberfiction!" we have cried since 2009. Always the line, "An experiment in and celebration of new writing" has sat somewhere in the first paragraph.

We've had a thorough turnaround of collaborators too: In 2004 we were Bruce, Joseph, Equus and myself; Joseph and Equus left within days; by 2009 we had been joined by Leoba, David, John and Lois; by 2011 it was just me, which is part of the reason *TFF* took a year's hiatus. Now, as of 2015, we are joined by Regina, Kathryn, Tracie, Valeria, Cécile (who has illustrated stories since 2006), Serge; plus Lori and Fabio who have guest-edited anthologies and continue to be valued collaborators.

We have attracted a fabulous team of artists, a critical and generous cohort of reviewers, and a community of support that we plug into via social networks and occasional conventions. We've had a huge amount of support, both financial and in-kind, during the crowdfunding campaigns for the last three anthologies, and we engage both productively and cordially with several other small presses, publications and writing communities. In 2005 it was mostly me, sketching and photoshopping, reviewing whatever junk I found lying around, bribing and threatening people to send us their stories, funding the whole thing out of my pocket.

I measure the success of *TFF* by such intangible things—legends who turn out to have heard of us; people who can publish professionally nonetheless sending us their stories; the generosity and excitement of new and potential collaborators. But if you want more measurable criteria, no less than eight stories first published in our pages have been shortlisted or honorably-mentioned in awards and year's bests; ten stories have been reprinted in some of the most prestigious and high-quality anthologies such as Gardner Dozois's *Year's Best*, Lethe Press's *Heiresses of Russ*, the Apex *World SF* and Mammoth's *SF Stories by Women*.

We hope to drive this success ever onwards. Our aim has always been to publish progressive ideas, underrepresented voices, socially important stories, and people clearly think that's a worthwhile goal. We've learned a lot about what all of these mean over the years as well—learned to check our own privilege and be much more sensitive to issues of gender, race, class, ability, language, and so many other facets of oppression. We're able to be selective now on features above mere quality, fit and taste; *in addition* we filter by features such as respect, not punching down, lazy stereotypes that we might have missed before we had such an inclusive team able to share their judgements of privilege and oppression with us.

But we've also always wanted to have fun, to push the boundaries, to play games that Borges, Kafka, Calvino and Eco would be tickled by, and people seem to enjoy that too. We feel it's important to treat authors and artists with respect, which among other things means paying them properly for their work, and we have some ideas for improving our finances to do better on that front in the future.

But most importantly, my co-editors Valeria and Cécile have done a great job helping put together this anthology of old and new stories, and we hope you enjoy reading them. If you do, keep coming back to **futurefire.net**; we plan for there to be plenty more where these came from!

Nasmina's Black Box

Jennifer Marie Brissett

Her name was Nasmina. Her mother combed and braided her hair into a multitude of plaits that jutted off her head every which way. The ends finished with pastel colored clips, making her look like a short brown court jester—especially when she jumped up and down, which she often did when excited about something.

Nasmina was the daughter of a great fixer. Her Dada could fix anything that broke down, from toasters to computers. And in the heat and humidity of the Caribbean island where her family lived, all machines would fail sooner or later. Nasmina's father wasn't some simple tinker. In many countries he would have been considered an inventor, or even a genius, but there on a small island where the surf greets the sand in washes of salt and white spray, he was simply called a fixer. The villagers knew his value, respected him, and treated him well. Life for Nasmina and her family was humble on the island. And that was just fine by her Dada.

In the month when Nasmina turned six she was finally allowed to go inside her father's workshop. It had long been a forbidden place, since her fingers were too eager to touch things that weren't hers. After much begging and pleading, she finally convinced her Dada of her restraint and he allowed her into this most secret and magical of places. So many wonders existed in that shack. Wonders that she was told were to never talk about with anyone. Her father made her swear to keep her lips still about all she had seen. And she swore and crossed her heart.

It was a small shack built in the backyard near the entrance of the old rainforest that lay just beyond their property. Even though there were only three walls to the shack, the workshop remained cool inside as her father had invented an air conditioner that didn't need to have the room enclosed. During the day the shack stayed open towards the rainforest and at night her Dada and her brother Jessem dragged a corrugated tin sheet to lean against the side to cover the shack closed.

The cool ocean air permeated every aspect of life on the island. It drifted high and low and spun around and around, caressing the skin and making brightly colored dresses on stocky women wave. The same breeze blew through the workshop as Nasmina was given the grand tour. In that shop her Dada had turned cans and the contents of an old radio into a mobile radiation emitter to catch fish. With parts from a broken TV and an old computer, he had made a unit that displayed a life form that her Dada said existed outside of our dimensional space, though he had to admit he wasn't quite sure whether it was a creature from the past or the future. Her brother leaned against a table as his little sister gasped at their father's work. Jessem was lucky. He had been apprenticing with his father for almost two years. In that time Jessem had grown to be a bit taller than their father and was showing signs that he shared more than just their father's smile, but his brilliance as well. He was well pleased that his little sister could finally see their workspace. It was like letting a little elf in on a delicious secret.

Her Dada had even made a satellite receiver with which he secretly monitored the government's communication. It's important to watch "di president and di Tontons," he said, then he made a face of disgust.

"What are Tontons?" Nasmina asked.

"Tontons are demons that live in the city," her brother answered. "They have goat-like horns that turn about their ears and walk hunched over on hooved feet." Jessem bent his back and demonstrated.

Nasmina narrowed her eyes and folded her arms across her chest. She knew that Jessem sometimes liked to tell tall tales.

"It's true, Nasmina," Jessem said. "The Tontons are very dangerous. They are terrible, terrible, and you should run if ever you see one."

"Jessem, stop," their father said, seeing how frightened his little girl had become. "They only stay in the city," he said to Nasmina. "They would never come here."

"They don't like us," Jessem said.

"Why don't they like us?" Nasmina said.

"Di president and his people think we are different," her Dada said. "We, here on di countryside, come from different roots, different ancestors. But fi we be di same, Nassie. Don't let no one tell you no different. We di same people. We all human beings."

Nasmina and her brother shared a bedroom. Jessem kept a desk in the corner that Nasmina did not go near, knowing that her brother kept his secrets there, though in the past she had been known to take a peek or two.

"Little Shadow," her brother called (that was his name for her), "I want to show you something." He turned around from his desk. Jessem held out a small black box. "Now that you are old enough to go into Dada's workshop you are also old enough to see this." He opened the box and it was filled with connected wires, gears, and little glowing red, green, and yellow lights.

"This is my special project. Not even Dada knows about it."

"What does it do?"

"It makes things invisible."

Nasmina scrunched her face. "Are you lying to me? Dada says not to tell lies."

"I am not lying!" he said, his face serious and hurt (with a slight smile). Nasmina couldn't tell if he was playing or telling the truth.

"Here, hold it and turn the switch." He gave it to her. It was slightly heavy in her hands and warm. She could feel the gears moving inside after she turned the switch.

"Is it working?" Nasmina asked.

"No," he said with disappointment. "I can still see you. You only faded a little. I had it working for a while on smaller things. It's no good for things as big as you. I need to work on it some more."

"You will get it working," Nasmina said encouragingly. She felt guilty for having doubted him.

"Maybe," he said. "The problem is the batteries. They always run out before I have time to figure out what is wrong with it."

"I can get you batteries."

"Little Shadow, these are no ordinary batteries. I make them myself out of a metal I found. I need to find some more. The place where I get it from has very little left." He reached into the top drawer of his desk and pulled out a strip of the metal that was the heart of this homemade battery. It was copper-colored with a bluish tint and tiny flecks within the material sparkled as they caught the light.

"Have you ever seen this material?"

"All the time," Nasmina almost lied. It's not like she hadn't seen the material somewhere before. She just couldn't remember where that somewhere was. She made her face firm and confident so as not to reveal her uncertainty. Her brother looked skeptical.

"I'm going to make a battery right now. Want to see?" Nasmina jumped in the affirmative, bouncing up and down so that her barrettes clicked together.

She watched her brother as he dropped metal shards into a small thick metal bowl. He set a small burner aflame underneath the bowl and waited minutes as his metal turned into a golden goo. Nasmina held her arms tightly behind her back and craned her neck to peek over her brother's shoulder while he worked. With a thick potholder glove he poured out the liquid metal batter into a handmade mold to form his battery.

Nasmina felt proud to be a part of the great invention that her brother was making. His black box sat open on his desk with wires and things pulled out of it. Jessem left his battery to cool and reached into his desk drawer to take out a notepad and began to write. He wrote on the notepad what looked like squiggles with numbers and symbols that Nasmina couldn't read or understand. Then he turned to a fresh page and began to sketch. Nasmina watched as he made a stick figure with spindly antennae coming out of the head.

"Little Shadow, this is you."

"No, it's not!" she giggled and punched his arm.

"Yes, this is you," he laughed and continued to draw. He put arms and hands on the figure and drew a box in its hands. Then he sketched a wide circle around the figure.

"This is how my box will work. It creates a distortion field around itself that will cause light to pass through so that everything within a radius will seem invisible. It will be a very useful tool one day. That is, if I can get it to work."

"How do you find the box when it's invisible?"

"I try to remember where it is and feel around for it. Besides, the battery usually runs down before too long and it reappears."

"Is Dada helping you?"

"No. This is my own project. I want to surprise him with a working prototype. So don't tell him about it." But the real reason Jessem didn't want his Dada to know about the box was because he wasn't sure that it would ever work. He wanted to make his Dada proud or maybe, truthfully, he wanted to make him jealous. Dada was a very smart man and Jessem wanted to show him that he was clever, too.

Their Dada was completely self-taught. There were books all over the house that Dada had read, but mostly he learned from doing things and figuring things out. He had gone overseas once in his youth and came back within a few years proclaiming that "a'foreign" had nothing to teach him. His new bride back then—Mumma now—always thought that he had some bad dark experience out there that he was never willing to talk about. They settled in a tiny house on a parcel of land far on the outskirts of their hometown, intending to live out their lives quietly. The shack of wonders seemed to be enough for their Dada. It wasn't for Jessem.

"One day, Little Shadow, I want to go a'foreign and learn in one of the great universities."

"Dada says that they have nothing to teach."

Jessem smiled. "We will see."

For many months Nasmina stood guard to the entry of her Dada's workshop. She did her job diligently, accepting the orders of desired customers and turning away those people who only sought to waste her Dada's time. (Especially that chatty-chatty woman from down the road, who Nasmina was told to always say that her father was very busy.) She was always polite, but firm with adults despite being a six-year-old.

Nasmina sat on a grassy hill that you had to cross in order to reach her home. The grass had grown tall enough to reach the back part of her shins. Yellow wildflowers surrounded her on all sides of the hill. Nasmina liked to pick the flowers there and count their petals. She would count petals and wait for the customers to come. Nasmina held her knees folded close and hugged her legs and tried to remember where she saw her brother's strange metal. Was it on the beach? Nasmina thought hard, picturing all the places along the beach where she was sure to go. No, it wasn't there where she had seen the metal. Was it in the marketplace? She thought of all the stalls and the big women who spread their baskets of fruits and vegetables on the long tables to sell. Her auntie had a stall there and sometimes Nasmina would visit and taste the sweet, sweet mangos from her table. No, not there. Then where? Where did she see that metal?

Then one day Nasmina remembered. It was by the old green forest. She used to like to visit this place before her mother found out and told her the story about children disappearing in the forest never to be seen again. There was a small river that ran by a tuft of trees whose water was clear and tasted light and refreshing like melon juice. It was at the place where the water came bubbling out of the rocks that she saw this metal. Not much of it but there would be enough to satisfy her brother's needs for a while. She made up her mind that as soon as she had the chance she would go into the old forest and find the metal for her brother.

At high noon, when the sun sat firmly in the sky, it became very hot. That was the time when Nasmina could come inside the shack to escape the mid-afternoon heat. There her Dada's many clocks would each click-clack and chime in their own unique way, ringing in noonday. The feed from the government receiver droned on about the cost of bananas and the foreign exchange rate while Jessem worked on a watch repair job and Dada worked on a circuit board. Nasmina sat near her Dada observing his nimble fingers twist a wire and solder a lead. He blew on the new connection gently to help it cool and solidify. Then he placed the prongs from a scope to the wires he had connected to the circuit and saw the signal wave it created on the scope's screen.

He touched a screwdriver to turn a pin on the circuit, which made the wave on the screen grow. Nasmina's big eyes widened even more as she observed the signal wave change by her father's slightest move. He made the signal wave peak and trough so high and so low that the wave appeared like vertical lines. Then when he turned the pin all the way down the wave became a flat undulating line.

The announcer who had been speaking in a monotone over the airwaves stopped in mid-sentence and was interrupted by a rushed voice. Then silence. The sudden lack of mundane chatter sent a cold shiver across Nasmina's forearm.

"Dada?" Nasmina asked.

"Shh!" her father said and put up his had for her to be still. They waited for the next words from the announcer that never came. The national anthem played instead and so it remained.

"What does this mean, Dada?" Jessem asked.

"I don't know. You two, please go inside. I will call for you later."

His children did as their father asked, but wondered and worried. Dada called for Jessem later as the rain began to fall. Nasmina watched them through an open window working in the backyard behind the shack. They spent an hour or more digging in the earth even as the rain came down in sheets of white. Nasmina saw them go back and forth from the shack, bringing out their father's best inventions and burying them in the hole they dug. Jessem and father came inside wet and covered with mud on their clothes and hands. No one said anything. The men washed up for dinner in silence. Mumma had made her best stewed chicken, and rice and peas with gravy. It was Nasmina's favorite dish. She only picked at it. Mumma would normally trouble Nasmina to not waste food, but tonight she said nothing and waited for Dada to speak.

The rain eased and fell now only in modest drip-drips that bounced off the corrugated tin roof, making a gentle rhythmic ting. It sounded like a sad song made on purpose for the occasion.

After listening to several bars of the tune, Mumma finally asked, "What is happening?"

Dada could not dismiss her like he did the children. He finally answered, "Di Tontons are on di move."

"Di Tontons? Will they come here?" Mumma asked.

"I don't know," Dada said. "Tomorrow I will try to find out more."

Nasmina dreamed that night. In a dream Nasmina saw herself. She was herself and then she was outside herself. She was her, yet someone else. She spoke to herself in conversation, giving advice and then warning. The words were hard to hear for their truth and then hard to remember as they began to fade. In this dream Nasmina was walking down her hill. Then, as it is in dreams, she was suddenly all the way back in her home just outside the green forest. She saw herself not as the little girl that she was, but as someone else who wore her favorite flowered shirt and her most comfortable knee-length denim shorts, the ones that were like her brother's.

The dark forest gave Nasmina shivers. She saw what she thought was a Tonton among the trees. It had curled, twisted horns that turned about its ears, flaring nostrils, and eyes a red burning flame. Then the image faded, as did her fear. She had to go inside, for her brother's sake. Her heart beat fast as she got closer and closer to the rainforest that stood menacingly deep and dark as an open grave against the blue Caribbean sky. Nasmina looked around carefully to make sure that her Mumma would not see her and then she entered.

She walked along a familiar path. It was as she remembered it (because in dreams everything is familiar). She approached a brook and followed it until she got to the place where the water came bubbling out of the rocks. And there she saw the flecks of the blue-green metal loosely embedded in the rocks at the bottom of the water. She scooped some into her hand. Then she was out in the sunlight with her brother's metal. Her brother would be so pleased. She shook with glee. She shook and shook and shook...

"Nasmina, wake up," her brother hurriedly whispered as he shook her by the arms.

He covered her mouth so she couldn't make a sound. The moon shined brightly through the window of their shared bedroom as if it were the sun. It was full and heavy against the dark blue night.

"You must be very quiet," he said. "There are Tontons in the yard."

Jessem picked up his sister and placed her in the bottom of the closet among his shoes.

"Take this," Jessem whispered and handed her his black box. "Hold this for me and do not let it go. No one will see you. You must stay very quiet, Little Shadow. They cannot see you, but they can hear you."

She nodded with her eyes wide like white orbs in the blackness of the closet.

"Stay in here, Nasmina, and don't come out until I come get you."

She was surrounded by her brother's clothes. They smelled of him. His shoes rested uncomfortably against her bare uncovered legs. He shut the door and all was black. Nasmina heard voices. Her Mumma and Dada spoke. Something tumbled. Then a slap. The voices were loud then distant. The closet door suddenly opened. A dark man stood before her and looked right at her. He held a gun. It was big like in the movies. He stared into the closet for a heartbeat more. In that moment Nasmina was not sure if her brother's box really worked. Then the Tonton shut the door as if he had seen nothing but the dark and stomped away. The slam of car doors. The sound of a vehicle leaving. All was so quiet then. The Tontons looked nothing like what her brother said. They were just men. Evil men with guns.

Nasmina stayed in the closet. She was silent and still and watched the moonlight turn to day through the crack where the edge of the door almost met the wall. She waited and waited for her brother to return. She waited as her bowels ached with the urge to go to the bathroom. It was so quiet. She feared to leave her hiding place. Then she remembered that she held her brother's black box. No one would see her if she left the closet. She could go to the bathroom and no one would know.

She timidly opened the door and looked around. There was no one. She crept out of her bedroom and into the hall. Still no one. She made her way to the bathroom where she relieved herself. She did so as quietly as possible and left the toilet unflushed so as not to make a sound. She knew her Mumma would chastise her for this later. She would explain that she was scared. Her Mumma would be mad for a while, but she would understand.

Nasmina held her black box and walked around the house. "Where did everybody go?" she asked herself. Outside was all quiet, even the birds. The sky was gray-blue and the sun struggled to peek through. Nasmina decided to go to town to find her auntie. She could stay with her until her Mumma and Dada and Jessem came home. That's what her Mumma always told her to do if ever she was lost. Go to auntie's stall in the marketplace and wait for Mumma to come get her.

She made her way down the road to town holding her brother's black box. Nasmina knew the way. She had walked it many times with Mumma and sometimes with Jessem. There were bushes and trees that lined the road. She thought she saw something in the bushes. Something wrong. She didn't stop to look. Nasmina kept walking, silent as a lamb and as quick as a thrush. She passed the beach, which was on her way. There were people sleeping on the beach. Lots of people. It was strange. They were unmoving but for their clothes which waved about in the breeze. Nasmina approached a man. He was still and covered in brown sauce. His eyes were closed and he had a deep cut on his side so that Nasmina could see his pink insides. She stepped back. She felt cold. She knew he was dead. They were all dead. Nasmina looked all around and pulled her brother's box to her chest. Then she ran as fast as she could. She ran and ran and didn't stop.

The market was silent. It was never silent. The fruits and vegetables were all mashed up. The stalls and tables turned over and strewn about the street. People lay with their exposed limbs in brown sauce. She didn't want to find her auntie's stall anymore. Nasmina wanted to go to the church. She would find the priest. He would know where Mumma and Dada and Jessem were. He would know what to do.

At the church, she pushed the front door open. The heavy door closed behind her. It was full with people in and about the pews. Brown sauce everywhere. And stillness. Nasmina walked along the aisle near the multicolored window. She knew these people. These were her people.

The church door opened and a Tonton came in. He wore a green uniform with a red beret. He carried in his hand a machete like her father had for cutting down the sugarcane that grew near their backyard. He sauntered about looking at the dead people. Then he saw Nasmina. Her body stiffened and she held tighter to the black box. The Tonton's jaw went slack in surprise. Then he slowly swung his machete onto his shoulder and backed out of the church.

Nasmina's throat was dry. She felt an itch on her face. She scratched at it and found that it was a tear. She wiped her cheek with the back of her hand and looked around. Something snapped in her mind. She didn't want to be in the church anymore. Silently she crept to the church door and opened it a crack. Outside she could see the priest talking to the Tonton. They spoke quietly and then they laughed together as if one had told a joke. The priest's long lean fingers gestured as he spoke, like they did during services. Nasmina watched them for a while, then the priest said goodbye, got into his car, and drove away.

Nasmina felt the hum and warmth of the black box in her hands. The batteries would run low soon and she would be seen. She needed to go to the place where she could find the metal for her brother's battery. Maybe that was where her family went. To the green rainforest where the trees grew tall like the pillars of a great cathedral. To the place where the sun was blocked out by large green leaves. She could find the brook and follow it to the deepest part of the forest.

She opened the door of the church and walked out. The Tonton turned and held his machete. His face twisted, but he didn't move. Nasmina held tight to her black box and turned towards the road. She was going to the rainforest to find the babbling brook where the flecks of blue-yellow metal under the water that comes out of the rocks. To the heart of the forest where no one else knew where she could be found.

The Taste of Their Dreams

Margo-Lea Hurwicz

Their ships appeared on the horizon. Their sails had captured the wind and were drawn to our home place. They landed on our shores. They came down from their ships.

They were the first; we had never had visitors before, and we were curious.

First they sent anthropologists, who wanted to study us.

They tried to speak to us, but we did not answer.

They drew symbols in the sand, and still we did not understand.

But when they slept, we entered their dreams.

We saw their world, heard their music, and tasted their longing.

They hungered and thirsted for otherness, and we were the other.

Dark after dark we watched them.

We learned to use their words and we spoke to them on their waking.

We told them our stories. We shared our best dances. We brought to them gifts of feathers and foodstuffs.

We thought they were like us.

We tasted their dreams and grew hungry for their dreaming. They showed us new colors; they played us new harmonies. They blended the flavors of their memory with the newness of our home place.

We did not taste danger.

We set dream-traps to lure them, to keep them in dreams.

Some fell to our dreams-traps, and they did not waken. They wanted to stay there. They languished and died.

The others grew frightened. They tended and guarded.

They came here to conquer, but at night we consumed them.

We sought not their dying, but we wanted their dreams.

Their numbers soon dwindled. They did not know why.

They packed their belongings and abandoned their shelters.

They sailed over the edge of the world and rose up to the stars.

Many cycles and cycles, and then they returned.

This time they sent archaeologists.

Where their shelters once stood, the site was littered with the cracked bones of the dreamers. Near the remnants of their ancestors, they built a new camp.

They lit fires and made music.

We waited for darkfall.

Shadow Boy and the Little Match Girl

C.A. Hawksmoor

21st September 1898

It has been almost a month, and every night the silence within me grows a little deeper. I will not be able to keep her job at the match factory for much longer. I am too clumsy. My mouth aches, and my hands are badly burned. I do not have her knack for the work, and do not know how we will survive this if she does not return. If anything happens to us, then it gives me a strange comfort to know that the truth of the matter will be written here. Words, at least, are more comfortable to my hands than phosphorus.

I do not know how to start. I have always been with her. The shadow that lies in the lee of her thoughts. I cannot tell you what it is like to grow up within a body that is not your own. I have never known another way.

Neither of us have ever fully understood what I am: a life that she has lived before, or one that has not yet come to pass. Whether something happened to her while she lay within her mother (or in years too distant into childhood to recall) to split her mind open like a gemstone with the Match Girl on one side, me on the other, and between nothing but a faceted surface full of stars. Perhaps she just dreamed me into being when she was very small, or found me one day in the park—nestled beneath the knotted brambles, in the coal-dust and very close to evening, shivering, and alone. Perhaps she made a home inside herself for me, because there was no other I could turn to.

However we came to pass, we are now as we are, and it cannot be undone.

It was always me that her father caught reading in a dark corner of the communal library on long and rainy afternoons. I looked at him with her eyes and he would tell me to go and play, which I quickly understood to mean that I should leave and give his daughter back to him.

It was easier with the other children: among the chimney-sweeps, piecers and hackers of the city's howling factories and humming servers. They would laugh, and run away from me when I came into her body as though they were afraid, but then they glanced back and shouted:

"Hurry up, Shadow Boy!"

Their voices like struck metal as the evening glinted in waves of golden fire on the clouds. Against the hulls of the solar ships drifting vast and black above us. And I ran after them.

Some of them played at having little shadows of their own. For all I know, those faces-behind-faces were as real as I am now. But they are not here any more. They belong amongst the dead.

To ensure I did not join them, I learned exactly when and how to hide.

23rd September 1898

My enduring memories of our adolescence are of the inside of her room. The clematis that wended its way beneath her window: the smell of its blossoming in summer, and the dull creak of its branches as her father's tabby tom cat climbed up through the tangled dark to curl beside me on her bed while I was at my reading.

Each night, she sat down at her worktable and breathed out deeply, banishing herself to the star-filled void between us and allowing me to come into her body. Each night, I opened that window to let the night air in over her skin. I sat down on her bed, opened my book, and waited for the cat to come calling somewhere after midnight.

From time to time, I dressed and crept out into the night instead. The gas lamps lit a path for me from the end of her street, all the way to the great shadow of the parkway. Skirting the liminal space between the carefully-mown lawns and the scuffling, wild darkness of the woods, I breathed in right down to the bottom of my belly. I began to forget about the strangeness of her body. I moved like a thing formed from the night itself, whilst the trees stood their silent vigils all around me: inverted creatures, wearing their lungs on the outside.

From the edge of the woodland you could see down rolling hillside all the way into the city, so long as the night was clear and the smog didn't hang too low. These were the years when they were still building the Algonquin Tower. From my vantage point, it looked like a great, broken tooth protruding from the city: its lower floors all lit up glass and neon green, floodlights pouring from its crown and catching against the underbellies of the clouds. Men and women labouring through day and night amongst the jagged cranes of their barren, concrete landscape. I would stare down at that glowing spire nestled amongst the smokestacks, with the cold wind on my cheeks and nothing to break the silence but the occasional clatter of a carriage heading down the main street and into town.

Both she and I came to the park as children (her skirts all dirty around the hem, and me occupying a space beside her that only she could see), but now it had become my domain alone. I have never known where she goes when I am in her body, only that I never see her and hear her the way she does with me. Perhaps it's simply that she rests silent, but I have always suspected that when I am here, she is not. That she goes to somewhere that I cannot perceive or understand.

Perhaps there are other creatures out there as I am, but she never speaks of it when she returns.

28th September 1898

She was a little over seventeen when she began writing letters to Zachary, whose name means 'Our Lord Remembers'. His parents went up to live in the first Lunar settlements years before he was even conceived, and all he had known of the our world was the earthshine. A distant curve of blue-green on the horizon, marked with the great, white swirls of slowly-moving weather. They were both so young. Enchanted to find an existence so completely alien from their own.

She understood from the beginning that he was sick. That some combination of his own biology, the Lunar gravity, and the strange networks of copper wire and silicon that the moonfolk graft into their brains and into their bodies, was killing him. But my Little Match Girl was too young not to hope, and so she would keep writing him her letters, and some nights I would put down my book and walk down to the airstrip to see the ships that whisked those letters up into her moon boy's hands. The airfield was brighter than the day in the white and sulphurous light: the ships hanging motionless above the gravity engines, connected to the ground by long, thin thorns of twisted metal. They looked like black clouds, snagged straight out of the sky.

She grew sick with devotion. And, as she sickened, he grew well. It was as though she had drained the poison out of him, and he began to flourish beneath her grace. We spoke less, and simply continued to divide night and day between us as we had always done. But she spoke to him of me, and he even wrote me letters once or twice: physical things made of paper and ribbon and bearing my name on the front that sent a strange thrill through my entire body, as though they had made me into flesh and bone in a way that nothing else had ever done. I wrote back in my own quiet, cursive hand. I tried to explain how the letters made me feel, but I do not think he understood.

3rd October 1898

It is in the nature of all living things to die. The sick and old are drawn to it as into the dark centre of a star. Passing through the heart of creation, into eternity. Amen.

And so it was with Zachary, whose name means 'Our Lord Remembers'. She loved him to the very limit of her being, but it was not enough to sustain him forever. The more she cried, the more silent he became. His letters came, shaky and infrequent, and then one day not at all.

She called to me then as a flame calls out to still, cold water. As she had not called out since we were children, and afraid. I was with her when she lit the white candle on her worktable, and over every night that followed I would see that it did not go out: trimming the wick, and passing the flame between the pooling wax of the old candle and the fresh ones that she brought home with her from the market.

I lay beside her in the dead still of the night, when I breathed out so deeply and allowed her to pass back into our body to sleep. She cried often, but even more than that she lay there in the dark, and stared up into nothing at all.

Eventually, one evening as I prepared to take her over and see to my evening rituals, she told me that she wanted me to stay. I understood her reasons. The world had become too hard. Too cold. Filled with no light but the tiny pool of liquid gold around the pale candle on our desk. A week, perhaps. Or maybe two. A little time immersed in the shadows and the stars of whatever place she visited when she was not within me. Then things would get better.

That was the end of August, and I have not heard her voice since. It does not seem to matter how hard that I call out to her.

12th October 1898

I thought it best to try and construct some kind of life here. I cannot sustain hers well enough on my own. I can only hope that when she comes back, the people and the things she cares about will come back to her, in turn.

Her clothes do not hang right, and I do not feel myself in them. I have no idea what will happen if I cease to be myself now she is not here, but I do not wish to find out. I bought some button-down shirts from a man in the market, and traded a few of the Match Girl's little wooden carvings for an old frock coat and a pair of pressed, black trousers.

I have been wearing her hair loose about her shoulders as I do, and a barber's boy from the city says that he can blacken it for me.

The streets are far busier in daylight, and I have tried to learn the subtle arts that people employ with one another as they go about their lives. I do not think that I have been very successful, although the situation is doubtless made harder by my unusual state of dress and strange way of speaking.

The working days are even worse, but I could only tell the master match maker that I was sick for so long. I need to survive here, so I must work.

The first day that I arrived dressed as I am, the match maker told me that she did not care who I was, or how I came to be. If I wanted to come into her workshop then I would wear a boned stay and an apron like the other girls. She gave me a bundle of clothes, and refused to let me work until I changed.

I must have struggled with the lacings for almost half an hour before Emily came back to see what was keeping me. She found me crying, angry, and humiliated. I should have found it simple. The other side of my mind had a hundred thousand tiny memories of how to do these things. But these memories belong to the Match Girl. They are not in my muscles or my fingers.

Emily helped me dress, and pinned my hair until I was not like myself at all. She did not understand why I would not stop crying, but she was kind with me. She calls on me each morning to help me dress, but I do not think that her kindness will matter for much longer. The memories of how to work with phosphorus and wood are as alien to my hands as the lacings of that dress.

The match maker shouts and corrects my work, and I burn my fingers often.

21st October 1898

I lost the job in the workshop, and have started an employment in one of the tiny noodle factories nestled beneath the eves of one of the housing towers on the north side of the city that has its highest reaches forever in the smog. It rains every day, and the only other things I notice as I go about my work are the rats that scurry through the corners of the room, and the slow dripping of cold water.

In the evenings, I prowl the cemetery grounds around the mausoleum just outside the south gate. I'm not sure what I am looking for.

I tried to ask the match maker if she would give my Match Girl her job back when I am no longer here. She did not answer. I do not think that she knew how.

31st October 1898

You can see the spire of the Algonquin Tower from the edges of the cemetery. It projects itself up into the night sky like a single note, held unwavering and forever in steel and green light. Perhaps I should not be coming here, but the park has become too loud and too close to the light to do the work that must be done within myself.

I cut between the leaning gravestones and the weathered angels: their edges all smoothed away, the faintest memory of wings still folded at their backs and the echo of hands clasped tight against their chest. The empty, rain-smoothed spaces where their eyes should be watching me. It is quicker to come this way, and meet the central avenue about a third of the way into the cemetery. There are long columns of two hundred year old oaks planted on either side of it, and by the time I reach avenue I cannot see the city through them. Not even the high peak of the Algonquin. I hear only the wrenching of the wind amidst the branches, and the slap of wet and amber leaves upon baked earth. The autumn drifts in heaps along that pale path, as it leads off between the trees straight into nothing at all.

It grows dark hours before I near the mausoleum gates, and by the time I see them looming up ahead there is no one for almost a mile around me. No one but the dead.

The gates have not been open in all the times that I have been there, and the old padlock chaining them together does not look as though it has seen use in centuries. I think the metalwork was white once, but time and rain and sootfall from the city has peeled paint from rusted metal and tarnished everything to lichen-green and chimney-black.

Beyond those gates, the great, granite pillars of the mausoleum seem to occupy eternity.

For years, people have come to this place to leave tokens for the dead. Maybe a few of them do it from some memory of whoever or whatever is buried in that awful place, but many more seem to come and remember those whose graves are far away, have been forgotten, or were never known to them. They tie ribbons bearing names, and weave bunches of dead flowers through the metal bars. They leave candles and offerings of perfume, bone and alcohol. Apples and pomegranates, poison mushrooms, and human hair. The foods and the things of the underworld.

Sometimes, I stay right up until the moment that the bells of St. Michael's chime the midnight hour, and I know I must go home and trim the wick of the white candle on her desk. See that the flame burns true.

I cannot allow it to burn out.

I read the names that are written on the ribbons, and listen to the gentle song of animal bones ringing against metal in the low wind. But most of all, I simply stare out into the void around the mausoleum. That close, it is a vast and pillared block against the sky: its thick, fluted columns wrapped in black and slapping ropes of ivy and echoes of graffiti decades old. The rabbits graze the grass around it low and soft, until it is like dew-covered velvet beneath the autumn moon. It looks as though you could sink into it for forever.

There are times when I think that I see her beyond those gates: running barefoot through that thick and moss-lined grass with her dress whipping at her heels. Laughing in a voice like the slow ringing of a bell. Skirting the shadows beneath the mausoleum as I once walked the narrow path between the parkland and the woods.

Every few steps, she turns around as though someone chases after her. But she never looks at me.

I do not think that she is coming back.

Flight of a Sparrow

Sequel to "The Birdwatcher" in *TFF* 29 (2014)

Jocelyn Koehler

"Raid confirmed," the voice on the phone warned. "Get him out."

"Acknowledged." Nia clicked off, and then chucked the phone into the compactor, where it was instantly crushed. It was cheap. Much cheaper than compromising communications. She'd get another one soon.

Nia looked at the stuffy room's other occupant. He was frail with age, his pale skin papery over thin bones. At the moment, he was fussing over a sparrow in a cage. One of his rescues.

"Time to go, Wally," she said. Nia felt weird calling him Wally. This little, quirky man was deeply linked into a system of activists determined to oppose an oppressive government. Nia didn't know details, but she knew his work annoyed the *hell* out of the powers that be. And her sole duty was to keep him safe.

She patted the pockets of her outfit. Pepper spray, metal keys. No ID, no gun. By orders, Nia wore scrubs, as if she were a medic instead of a bodyguard. Less obvious, sure. And certainly comfortable. But she didn't like how the fabric was powder blue, with cute little woolly sheep all over. Her skin looked even blacker against the light scrubs. *Scariest sister in pediatrics*, she thought wryly. Was the idea to make attackers die *laughing?*

"Ready." Wally picked up the cage and they headed for the door. Nia opened it first, scanning the hallway.

"Clear," she muttered. "Back stairs. Go."

They made it about two flights down when the thud of footsteps ricocheted up the concrete stairwell. Nia stopped.

"They're here already! Reverse," she ordered. "We'll go to the roof. I can hold—"

"Thinking like a bodyguard," Wally chided, but gently. "Don't panic. Take my elbow. Help me walk down."

Nia shook her head. She was trained in seven martial arts, but these were armed agents approaching. She was tough, but not that tough.

"Sir, I can't let you get caught."

"No *sir*-ing. Come on," Wally urged. "I've been up to no good for ten years, and never got caught yet. Trust me on this."

Nia took a deep breath, then reached to take Wally's elbow.

They kept walking, slowly. Wally seemed to age before her eyes, his steps hesitant, his gaze dulling. The bird twittered in its cage, unhappy with the jerky movements.

Agents rounded the corner a few seconds later.

They were caught.

Nia tensed, anticipating a fight. Orders to halt. *Something.*

"Out of the way!" the one in front said, not slowing down.

Nia yanked Wally to the side just before he was hit. "Watch where you're going!" she yelled at the agents.

Another one barely turned his head as they moved by. "Stand back, or you'll be interfering with a police action!"

"Oh, my!" Wally gasped. "Can we watch?"

"*No!*" the agent barked back. "Just... stay out of it!"

Nia tugged Wally's arm. "Let's go," she said. "We don't want trouble."

The agent watched them take a few steps down before turning back and following his group.

On the street outside, Nia sagged against the building. "They didn't even *see* us."

"They saw what we wanted them to see." Wally laughed. "An old fart and his nurse."

She looked at him. "So that's why you insisted I wear scrubs."

"In nature, it's called protective coloring. We look harmless, we blend in." Wally's chin rose. "And we survive."

Nia glanced up. "They'll be pissed when they don't find anything. Let's move. Safe house is a ways off."

He nodded, handing her the cage. Inside, the sparrow calmed down.

"Lead the way, Nia. Let's fly to our new nest."

What Hath God Wrought?

Neil Carstairs

There was no hint of warmth in the graveyard. A blanket of cold mist rested upon the land, layering ankle-length grass with dew and wreathing gravestones in a grey that resembled the misery of the departed. Captain James Milliner felt the cold seeping through his uniform and topcoat as he stood beside what had once been the last resting place of Pastor Oliver Jones. Now shreds of turf were scattered wildly around, some hanging from neighbouring gravestones like wigs. Earth from the grave lay in thick, wet clumps as if whoever had perpetrated this act had done so in a rush, with no care for neatness. A fact that came as no surprise to James, for within the hastily excavated grave was a splintered casket that had once held the Pastor, and within the casket was nothing but the cotton lining that had once comforted the body, and of the body, there was no sign.

James stood in the lee of the St John the Divine's Church; the dark stone edifice silent in its disapproval of the scene. This was desecration of holy ground and had no rightful place in the world. From somewhere out of sight a crow shouted its mournful call, as if the bird understood the transgression that had taken place.

"Witchcraft," Sir Joshua Salisbury said gruffly. He stood beside James and stared into the grave with the same mix of disbelief and horror. "That's what this is, Captain. Witchcraft."

James didn't respond. Salisbury wasn't from these parts; he had come from London with his florid cheeks, fat stomach and letter of authority signed by the Prime Minister. Sir Joshua was a Parliament Agent, with the powers to call to witness any man and the power, as James' presence here testified, to raise the militia. Sir Joshua sighed and walked away from the graveside, stopping only when he reached a gravel path.

"Damnable business," Salisbury said as James joined him. "Pastor Jones had been in his grave only a week before this happened. It's a blessing he was a bachelor and there is no widow to grieve twice over."

"How did he die?" James asked what he thought was a relevant question, considering the event that had taken place.

"His body was found in a field about two miles from the village. No evidence of foul play at the time. Now, however, I'm not so sure." Sir Joshua reached into his pocket and pulled out a folded sheaf of papers bound together by a silk ribbon. He held them out for James to take. "Lord Farley is the landowner hereabouts. He carried out the inquiry into Pastor Jones' death. This is his report."

Salisbury began walking slowly down the path towards his carriage that waited in the lane. James followed. Across the churchyard, about thirty yards away, the eight men he commanded took on the form of ghosts in the mist, the muted red of their uniforms gave the only colour to the scene. Salisbury said,

"Find who did this. Find out, too, if the Pastor's death was murder. It's a bad business, especially so soon after All Hallow's Eve."

"You believe it was witchcraft?" James asked.

"Witchcraft or madness, if there is a difference." Salisbury stopped to stretch his left leg. "Damned arthritis. It's the damp, you know. It gets into the joints and doesn't let go."

"It must be uncomfortable at this time of year," James said, sympathetically.

"Aye, it is, and the winters are longer and the summers are shorter than when I was your age. Something you may find out in thirty years time." Salisbury paused to study James. "I've heard good things about you. You are engaged, so I understand."

"Yes, sir, to Emma Cartwright, our marriage will be next summer."

"A nice girl, I know of her father through the Merchant's Board."

"He's a fine man," James said.

Salisbury laughed, a sudden burst of sound in the silent graveyard. "And soon to be your father-in-law, which of course has no bearing on your statement, does it?"

"Perhaps a little," James was honest in his reply.

Salisbury's face became serious again as they reached the gate. "Do your duty, Captain. I expect an honest appraisal of the situation. I'm staying with Bishop Hurd at Hartlebury Castle for a few days, and then return to London. If you need to discuss anything before presenting your report then have no hesitation in approaching me. These events can only provoke panic in the countryside. Your presence here will at least show the locals we are properly investigating matters."

Salisbury eased his bulk thought the gate. His driver had stepped down and now held a door open. The carriage swayed as Salisbury boarded it. The driver mounted quickly back to his place. As the driver cracked the reins Salisbury pulled back the window cover and said,

"Don't let me down, Captain."

James watched the carriage bounce away along the rutted lane. Winter rains had brought mud down from the fields and the road surface fought a losing battle to preserve its status. When the carriage took a turn in the lane and vanished from view James went back along the path and across the grass to where his men waited.

"We will be here two or three days," James said to Sergeant

Corbett. "Take the men into the village and find accommodation."

"Where will you stay, sir?" the sergeant asked around the clay pipe that hung from his mouth.

"Sir Joshua gave me the key to the vicarage. I will spend the night there and look around to see if there is anything that can assist us in our duty."

Corbett took hold of his pipe and used the stem to gesture towards the empty grave. "Are we looking for who did that?"

"Yes."

"And if we find 'em?"

"We take them into custody for transport back to Worcester, to appear before the assizes."

"And if they don't want to come with us?" the sergeant asked.

James looked at the muskets each man held before saying. "Then best keep your powder dry."

It was the first time James had ever stayed in a dead man's house and he hoped it would be the last. The first few hours, as winter daylight faded to night, he spent going through the Pastor's personal effects. He found nothing to suggest the man was anything other than a God-fearing Christian. Later in the afternoon James realised he was getting hungry. There was no food in the house worthy of that description so he walked down to the village and ate in a tavern called The Talbot. The meal was passable if he chewed the meat enough times and he then spent the next hour sipping at a jug of ale re-reading the report Salisbury had passed to him. Lord Farley had conducted the investigation into Pastor Jones' death and found no reason to record any ruling but death by natural causes. It was odd that Jones had been so far from the village, but the two men who discovered his body were deemed to be honest in their statements. James looked at the names. Thomas Brooke and Richard Cooper both lived in the village; he would question them in the morning. James finished his ale and returned to the vicarage. The house was dark and silent, and the lamp that James lit did little to dispel the gloom. It was as if the building was in mourning for its former occupier. James spent time in the study, looking at the bookshelf that dominated one wall. Jones had been well read; there were editions of Shakespeare, Milton, Chaucer and Johnson and philosophical texts by Locke, Spinoza and Hobbes. James flicked through the pages of a King James Bible but saw no hidden pentagrams or subtle sub-texts that would point towards the Pastor being a witch or Satanist.

James slept in an armchair in the study as the thought of occupying Jones' bed left a bad taste in his mouth. He woke early, his back and neck aching from the chair and waited until first light and before returning to the village. The landlord of The Talbot let him in and fed him a side of bacon and poached eggs. Sergeant Corbett and three of his men were there as well, looking the worse for drink. When their breakfast was finished James took Corbett to one side.

"I need to speak to two men. Thomas Brooke and Richard Cooper. Divide the squad into two, find each man and bring them separately to the place where they found Pastor Jones dead. They can guide you. Don't answer any questions if they ask."

Corbett nodded his head carefully, the pain in his eyes reflecting the hammer blows of his hangover. James left the militiamen and walked through the village. Yesterday's mist had lifted a little, giving him at least a partial view of the valley and floodplain below. James used the map in Lord Farley's report to guide him to the field where Pastor Jones had died. The neat line work showed the relationship between the village and the field. James followed the Tenbury road for two miles before turning off towards the river. Hedgerows bordered the lane he was on; birds flitted within the tangled branches and the redwings, sparrows and finches called to each other as he passed. He turned again, this time onto a bridleway, walking close to the hedgerow to stay away from the rutted mud that formed the central body of the path.

The map James was following showed the bridleway turning right to run alongside an area of woodland the cartographer had named Forty Acre Wood. It was at this turn that a gate into a pasture field gave James his first view of the place where Pastor Jones had died. James had been expecting something more than a flat area of grass. He had thought that perhaps there would be something else here, a reason to attract Jones to his death. James studied the map again, there was an X marking the approximate location where the body had been found.

Forty-Acre Wood bordered one side of the field, another side was bordered by the bridleway, and the River Teme ran along a third. James walked across grass that reached up to his ankles and felt the cold dew through the leather of his boots. He stopped where he judged that Jones' body had lain. There was nothing to give him any clue that death had visited this place. Grass grew in clumps and whatever animals had grazed here were now in winter quarters, somewhere warmer and safer from the possibility of flooding. James tucked the map away in a pocket and went to the river.

The Teme was running close to the top of its banks, water the colour of red mud swirled and eddied as it carried rain from the Welsh mountains. To James, the water mirrored his feelings. Why was he here? Sir Joshua had said he had heard good things about James. Did that mean he had been chosen for this duty? James shook his head. Was it because he was the son of a clergyman, or because he was a teacher? Did Sir Joshua believe James was better placed than any other volunteer officer in the militia because of his background? James watched as the remains of a tree, caught in the fast moving current, swept past. He turned from the river to look back at the field. A shadow on the ground caught his attention, off to his right and well away from the entrance to the field. From his point of view it just looked like a dark line on the surface of the grass, as if a lone plough furrow had cut through the sod. As much because he had little else to do, as he was intrigued, James walked to the shadow. The dark area took shape, filling out from a line to an ellipse to eventually form a circle. He stopped at the edge. The grass was flattened, as if a heavy object had lain upon the turf, and also discoloured. James squatted, plucking a few stalks and holding them up for closer inspection, it seemed to him that the grass stems had been drained of colour. He pulled a handful up, rubbing them hard between his fingers. A watery brown liquid that smelt of decay spilled out onto his skin.

James stood and examined the circle again. He didn't step into it, some nagging doubt made him careful. He paced around the circumference and counted each step. He reached ninety-three when he returned his start point, which, he calculated, made the diameter of the circle approximately thirty paces. James squatted again, the earth beneath the grass was moist, and he used his pocketknife to probe the surface but found nothing below to give a clue as to the condition of the grass.

A murmur of voices made James look up. James could see the shakos his men wore above the upper branches of the hedge, as the first group made its way along the bridleway. He went to meet them as they came through the gate. The escort stopped at the field entrance and allowed the man with them to walk on alone.

"Are you Thomas Brooke or Richard Cooper?" James asked.

"Richard Cooper, sir." The man seemed awed by James's gold epaulettes.

James studied Cooper; he was short and squat, some sort of labourer judging by the size of his shoulders. He wore wood-soled shoes and woollen cloth trousers and shirt.

"You found Pastor Jones here?"

"I did, sir," Cooper's eyes flicked to the areas where the body would have lain. He licked his lips nervously, not able to look James in the eye. For a moment Cooper's gaze slid past James towards the strange patch of grass.

"Tell me what happened," James said.

"Happened, sir?" Cooper frowned, as if the question made no sense. "We found him dead."

James took Lord Farley's report out of his pocket; opening the pages he found Cooper's statement. James pointed to a rough X at the bottom of the page.

"Is this your mark?"

Copper stared blankly at the paper. "Aye, it is."

"What happened to make you come here of all places in search of the pastor?"

"I…" Cooper fell silent. James sighed.

"When did Pastor Jones go missing?"

"About a fortnight ago."

"What happened when it was realised he was missing?"

Cooper shrugged. "His housekeeper went to Lord Farley. His Lordship called all the men of the village together and asked us to search for the Pastor."

"So you paired with Thomas Brooke?"

"Aye."

"And it states in this report that two hours after Lord Farley started the search you and Brooke reported finding the Pastor's body."

"If it says so."

"It does say so." Cooper still couldn't meet James' eyes. James said. "Follow me."

He led Cooper across the field to the circle of grass. Cooper looked at the ground, it seemed to James that the man shrank from the sight of the discoloured grass. James was silent, letting the weight of Cooper's thoughts press down onto the labourer's shoulders. James saw the next group of his men coming down the bridleway.

"Go and stand on the far side of this grass."

Cooper followed the order by walking around the perimeter and avoiding stepping on the strange grass. James went to meet Thomas Brooke. He didn't bother with any questions. He led the second man until they stood opposite Cooper. From somewhere in the woodland a group of crows set up a sudden cacophony of hoarse cries. Brooke shivered within his homespun clothing. James went to stand in the centre of the circle. He looked first at Cooper and then at Brooke.

"Come and stand by me," he said. Reluctantly, the two men came forward. They trembled as if they were frightened pups. James spoke quietly. "Tell the truth of that night."

Neither man reacted. James gave them time. He could hear the soft murmur of his men as they talked amongst themselves, he could hear the crows calling in the trees and he could hear the rush of floodwater in the river. Finally, he heard what he wanted, as Brooke spoke.

"We saw the Pastor in the village the night before. He was full of excitement, said he had seen a wondrous event and asked us to fetch weapons and go with him."

"You came here?" James asked.

"Aye, to this field."

"What was here?"

Brooke glanced at his friend for support. "There was a barrel here, where the grass is dead."

"A barrel?" James asked.

"A barrel, not like a barrel of ale but bigger, the size of a house and it was glowing like the moon."

"And there were men," Cooper interrupted in a rush, as if a dam had finally been broken and his words were water pouring through the breech. "Or what could have been men but weren't. They were the size of children, with big heads and thick bodies."

"What happened?"

"Pastor Jones told us to remain hidden," Brooke said, "and went out to speak to the... men. He got close to them when he fell to the ground and didn't move."

"We saw three of the men approach him. We thought they meant harm." Cooper shrugged. "We fired our muskets at them. One fell, the others fled back to their barrel and we saw it rise into the air. It had no wings and it had no sails but it rose like a bird into the sky until we couldn't see it no more."

Now it was James' turn to shiver. Neither man had the education, intelligence or imagination to invent such a tale. He looked down at his feet, at the ground he stood upon. What had rested here? He could not tell, and in some ways did not want to.

"Did you leave then?"

"No," Brooke said, shaking his head emphatically. "We went to the Pastor, but he were dead."

"And the other body?"

"The musket ball had struck it and as much as we could tell, it were dead too."

James knew the question he had to ask. "What happened to the other body?"

"We hid it in the hedge, just so's Lord Farley and his men didn't see it when they came to collect the pastor."

"Is it still there?" James turned towards the hedge, as if expecting the creature to reveal itself. Brooke and Cooper remained silent, staring at the ground in discomfort. James spoke quietly. "What did you do?"

"We had to move it. Lord Farley said he was coming back to the field and even in this cold the body might start to go rotten."

"Where did you put it?" James asked when they fell silent again.

"By then the grave for Pastor Jones had been dug. We went one night and brought the thing back to the churchyard, scraped out some more earth and put the body in. The Pastor's coffin went in on top and hid it."

James knew that he was out of his depth in this place, as much as he would have been if he had entered the river. He felt as if he was disconnected from the men and the field. The world around him was changing and he had no power over that change.

"You can return to the village," he told the two men, his voice harsh. "But I may need to speak to you again."

He let Brooke and Cooper walk away. Sergeant Corbett came forward to meet James. "Are you letting them go, sir?"

"For now," James watched as the villagers disappeared from view. "I have learnt something, though what it means I do not know."

James led the militia back to the village. He could feel their eyes on his back, questioning his actions, and he couldn't blame them for James too had some of the same feelings. When they reached the first buildings he called Corbett to his side.

"I need to consult with Sir Joshua, so keep the men sober tonight."

James hired a horse from the blacksmith and set out for Hartlebury. It took him the best part of four hours to reach the castle. James used the Holt ferry to cross the Severn and then went up the hill and through Ombersley. The castle had been the seat of the Bishops of Worcester for centuries. James felt a thread of apprehension as he rode into the wide quadrangle. He knew what he was going to say; he just did not know what reply he would get.

A stable lad took care of James' mount, and a liveried footman led him along corridors lined with portraits to a study where Sir Joshua Salisbury waited, a glass of port in hand. An open fire filled the room with comforting warmth. Across the room from Salisbury sat Bishop Richard Hurd, he greeted James with an inclination of his head.

"You have something to report, Captain?" Sir Joshua asked.

James felt his voice shake as he began. Now he was here the story sounded too incredible to be true, as if it were the ravings of a lunatic. When he finished Sir Joshua and the Bishop were both silent. Salisbury sipped at his port before he asked.

"So what do you believe happened in the churchyard, James?"

"I think the barrel and its crew returned to reclaim the body of their companion, and at the same time took the body of Pastor Jones as well."

Bishop Hurd moved as if driven to a sudden decision. He stood and sighed, walking to a mantelpiece where a folded sheet of paper lay. The Bishop opened the paper read silently before turning back. A look passed between Salisbury and Hurd, just a momentary glance that spoke more than a thousand words. James frowned as he felt a sudden twist in his gut; a burst of confusion at what he didn't understand and realisation of what he did. James took a breath of air as his heart began to race. They knew. Sir Joshua Salisbury, Parliament Agent, and Richard Hurd, Bishop of Worcester, knew about the barrel and the strange creatures that rode in it.

"Pastor Jones wrote to me over two months ago with a strange tale of a vessel with no visible means of propulsion," Bishop Hurd said. "I found it hard to believe, but Oliver was a sober man of good disposition and I had no choice but to give credence to his report. When he sent word again that the vessel had reappeared I made contact with Sir Joshua. We were on the point of further investigation when news came of Oliver's death. That changed our view."

"This vessel," Sir Joshua tossed his hand in the air as if he disliked the use of the word. "Any chance the people who crew it are French?"

"From what I was told, sir, I doubt even a Frenchman would look like this crew."

"Damn shame, if you beg my pardon Bishop," Salisbury grumbled. "We could do a lot by hanging this on the French."

"What do you make of this, James?" the Bishop asked.

"Make, sir?" James frowned. "I'm not sure."

"Come now, a young man with your background must have made some sort of deduction from the evidence you have heard. You have heard of the principle of Lex Parsimoniae?"

"Of course, your grace," James answered.

"Before today would you have believed in a vessel that could fly? We have two men who witnessed this and the written testimony of a third, a man of good character and education. When placed with such evidence what can we postulate now?"

Salisbury spoke from his chair. "That this vessel comes from either a land as yet undiscovered on this earth or from the heavens."

Hurd nodded and read from the pastor's letter. "The barrel rose into the night sky without sound, becoming smaller and smaller until it was lost to sight amongst the stars."

"It comes from somewhere else," James said.

"But where?" the Bishop asked. "From the moon or one of the planets, or from beyond even those astral bodies?"

"We are faced with a delicate and serious situation," Salisbury pushed himself from his chair and approached James.

"God made man in his own image, that is what the scriptures tell us," Bishop Hurd said. "So does this mean that God made these visitors as well? If not, who made them? And if they were not part of creation, then did creation take place?"

James felt his skin go cold. Salisbury saw the look on James' face and took his cue from it. "I still believe there is a link to the occult in all this business."

Bishop Hurd nodded. "I fear you may be right."

The Bishop reached down to hold Pastor Jones' letter out to the fire. Smoke rose briefly as the paper charred and then a flame took hold with a tongue of orange. The letter curled and blackened. The Bishop held on for as long as possible before letting the remains of the paper fall into the body of the fire. Flakes of ash were cast up, caught in eddies of air and swept into the chimney. James felt a part of himself go with them.

"No doubt a band of travellers were involved in this," Salisbury said. "Most likely they will have headed north. I shall have word sent to Shrewsbury to be on the lookout for these occultists."

"Which leaves us with the two remaining witnesses," the Bishop said.

Salisbury fixed James with a gaze as hard as stone. "We must defend the Church and the State, James. If news of this event became widespread it would signal the beginning of the end of all we hold sacred. What price a world that loses its faith? I am sure that you are as aware of this as we are, and because of that we will fully support whatever actions you have to take when you return to the village."

James waited for more, wanting Sir Joshua to spell out exactly what those actions might entail. The room remained still; dust motes turning in the winter sunshine that filtered through the leaded windows gave the only sign that this wasn't some strange waxwork tableau. James wanted to move but his legs refused to co-operate with his brain. As the seconds dragged by Sir Joshua tired of James' presence.

"Return to the village, captain. When we next meet I want this affair to be behind us."

James walked from the room on legs that were stiff with fear. Whatever help he had sought when coming to the castle he had not contemplated that Sir Joshua and Bishop Hurd would have already known about the strange visitors. The same footman who had led him to the study now took him back through the panelled corridors. The stable lad was waiting patiently and James automatically dropped coins into the boy's palm. He rode away from the castle and didn't look back. James stopped in Ombersley and bought bread and cheese which he ate as he rode. He watched the sky as he traced the roads back to he village. The clouds were breaking and a cool blue showed him a new view of the heavens. At night he would see the stars in all their glory, but what else would he see if he looked closely enough?

It was after nightfall when he reached the village. He found Sergeant Corbett in The Talbot, sitting in front of a tankard of ale. "I want all the men outside this inn before sunrise. Full uniform."

"Are we leaving, sir?"

"Not until we have finished our work here," James said.

"And what work might that be, sir?"

"Work that requires two lengths of stout rope," James spoke quietly. Corbett's eyes narrowed.

"Are we not going back to the assizes?"

"Not this time, sergeant," James said, and turned away before Corbett could see the fear in his eyes.

James returned to Pastor Jones' cottage. He slept in the same armchair, disturbed by dreams of flying barrels and strange men. James woke with a stiff neck and aching back. He shaved in a bowl of cold water and brushed the creases from his uniform before walking down to the inn. Corbett had the men out and ready for him. In the pale light of a lantern James inspected them before saying,

"We came here to investigate the death of Pastor Jones. I have interviewed two men, and consulted with Sir Joshua Salisbury and the Bishop of Worcester. We now have to carry out our duty."

Corbett had purchased rope from the innkeeper. James had already selected a good tree, an oak that stood just outside the village on the Bromyard road. He sent three men to ahead prepare the ropes and led the others to Thomas Brooke's house. Corbett banged on the door with the stock of his musket. Brooke appeared, half dressed with his hair tangled and eyes full of sleep. James had two men grab the labourer and tie his hands. Brooke's wife came to the door.

"Where are you taking him?" Her voice was shrill with fear, striking out into the twilight. The militiamen ignored her, tracing the narrow street to the cottage of Richard Cooper. A similar scene was enacted; Cooper came with barely any protest, he had no wife or family and so the cottage was left with its door open, as if the building was in shock at the treatment of its owner. The party marched through the village as dawn paled the horizon. At the oak tree the ropes were in place, looped over strong branches and noosed in readiness. Cooper and Brooke saw the ropes and knew what they meant. The two men began to protest, proclaiming their innocence, begging to be told of the charges brought against them.

"With the authority vested in me," James talked over their panicked voices, "I find you guilty of acts of murder and blasphemy. You will be hanged by the neck until you are dead."

It took five men to get the first noose over Brooke's head. He was hauled upwards, feet kicking and body twisting as the branch overhead creaked. James forced his eyes to remain on the hanging man; it took fifteen minutes for him die. By the end, only James was looking, his militiamen had turned away, facing outwards in a loose circle. Cooper was dragged forward next, his resistance had gone and it was as if he had already accepted his fate. A shout brought James' head round. A man dressed in the leather apron of a smith was running towards them. Two of the militiamen barred his way, muskets raised to reinforce their action. The smith retreated without another word, but the accusation in his eyes cut at James's soul as if it were a knife. James turned back to the tree to see Cooper weeping. James gave the signal and the oak protested again at the weight of another man was hung from its branches.

James waited until the sun had fully risen and he could be sure that Brooke and Cooper were dead before ordering his men to form up and march away from the village. There was none of the usual banter between the militiamen and James was glad of the silence. He looked down from the road towards the Teme, the sun showed the river as a silver ribbon threading through the drab winter landscape. James thought he could see the field where Pastor Jones had died and the strange marking on the ground. The secret of whatever had happened in that field was with Cooper and Brooke, and with Pastor Jones, wherever his body now lay.

Frost had formed on Chapter Meadows, across the Severn from Worcester Cathedral. James could see the sun sparkling on the grass like a thousand diamonds from the window of his lodgings. A trow made its way down the river, laden with goods bound for Bristol. James looked down at the recently delivered note in his hand. Sir Joshua Salisbury was returning to London and requested James' report to take with him. With a final look out of the window James walked to the secretaire that stood in one corner of the room. He sat, slipped a sheet of paper into position and stared at the blank page. He had barely slept in the two days since returning from the village. Each time he closed his eyes he saw the bodies of Brooke and Cooper swinging in the breeze, an image that would be with him for the rest of his days.

The chimes of a church bell brought him back to the present. James sighed, lifted his pen and dipped the nib into an inkwell. He hesitated; forming the words he would write in his mind, imagining Sir Joshua Salisbury reading them as he travelled south in the post coach. The nib descended and scratched a path across the surface of the paper.

I, James Milliner, Captain of Militia in the County of Worcestershire, do give oath, in the presence of Our Lord, this 17th day of November 1792, that the report I give is a true and honest one of Witchcraft in this County.

James paused in his writing to examine the words he had written. He felt his hand begin to shake and a droplet of ink fell from nib onto paper. He looked at the stain, and saw it not as ink but as a barrel, one without wings or sails, preparing to fly to some place unknown.

Fae Visions of the Mediterranean

Valeria Vitale

EXT. AIRPORT CAR PARK—DAY

In the frame there is a young MAN (early 30s) in the driver's seat of an average car, clearly waiting for someone. A WOMAN (late 60s) arrives and enters the car. They greet each other, the woman sits in the passenger seat, and the man starts the engine.

INT. CAR

The conversation takes place as he drives. He sometimes stops at traffic lights or changes gear, to break the monotony of the sequence.

> MAN
> Thank you so much for flying all the way down here. We really appreciate it.

> WOMAN
> I couldn't possibly miss my granddaughter's wedding.

> MAN
> (goofily)
> I thought sailors only travelled by sea.

> WOMAN
> What a silly idea!

> MAN
> Forgive me. I'm totally fascinated by the Mediterranean.
> (beat)
> Actually, I want to write a story about it. Maybe something... mysterious, you know?

> WOMAN
> Good for you.

> MAN
> So... Eh... If I may ask... Did you ever see anything strange when you were out there in the Blue?

WOMAN
Whatever do you mean, son?

MAN
Dunno. Something a bit... eerie, maybe?

WOMAN
Sure! Because on the Mediterranean we all secretly worship ancient gods and we all keep sirens in formaldehyde for our biology classes, right?

MAN
(chuckles uneasily)

WOMAN
(heatedly)
Do you want to hear something *strange*? I can tell you about the toxic waste in the port of Trieste. Or idiots pouring concrete on the coasts of Montenegro. Do you want a horror story? What about people shot to death when they try to leave Syria or Libya? *That* is fucking horrifying.
(speaking right in his face now)
Why don't you write a story where all the people drowned between Africa and Lampedusa come back to the surface and eat the heart of the bastards that shot them on the boats? Better: they don't even eat the hearts, they chew them and spit them in the waves.

MAN
Someone's getting carried away!

WOMAN
Whatever...

The woman takes off her light sweater. She wears a top underneath that reveals several tattoos. The man looks at them couple of times. The woman catches his eye.

MAN
Sorry! Didn't mean to stare.

WOMAN

No worries. If I had cared about people staring at me I wouldn't have inked my skin.

                    MAN
They look great! Mostly words. Are they in different languages?

                    WOMAN
                    (smiling)
Uh yeah. This is Italian, because this is where I came from. Oh, this one is Arabic. A souvenir of when I lived in Algeria. That's Greek. Old story. There is another one here, it's Corsican. Because we all make mistakes.
                    (grins)

                    MAN
That's really impressive! You understand all those languages?

                    WOMAN
A little, yes. Is it really impressive? I'm sure you know bits and pieces of many languages too.

                    MAN
Me? No! I only speak English. We are a bit spoilt! Everyone speaks some English, right?

                    WOMAN
That is quite dull.

The man's embarrassment sinks into silence. They drive.

                    MAN
We're almost there! I need to pick up my folks, I left them on the beach to enjoy the view of the sea. It's the first time they've ever seen the Med!
                    (smiles knowingly)

The man is about to open the door of the car, then he stops.

                    MAN
You know, I was really hoping you could help me with my story!

WOMAN
I wish I could! But, to be honest, I don't really understand what you're looking for. The Mediterranean is a pond. A giant bath tub. It's a place of work. Hard work. It's a liquid road, to go from one place to another. It's plenty of fish. And waste. That's it. Everything else is junk we sell to tourists.

MAN
(disappointed and vaguely humiliated)
I guess you're right.
(exits the car)
I'm going to find my family and bring them here. They're looking forward to meet you! Sofia has spoken so much about you! Do you mind waiting here for us?

WOMAN
Not at all. Take all the time you need. See you in a bit.

When the man disappears from view, the woman gets out of the car and walks towards the sea. The camera follows her and leaves the car behind. She takes her shoes off and rolls up her trousers. She takes a deep breath and closes her eyes, then she slowly enters the salt water.

ANGLE ON—WOMAN AND SEA FILL FRAME

WOMAN
My love. I missed you so much.

SHOT HOLDS AS CREDITS ROLL

Reflection

Jessica E. Birch

This is how it begins.

You open the carved cherry-wood shutters and gaze into the mirror. The skirt with its heavy midnight brocade, the high-heeled slippers pinching your feet, the viciously tight corset stealing the air from your throat like the hand of a jealous lover—they make you beautiful.

Beautiful?

Mirror, mirror, on the wall
Who is the fairest of them all?

You are.

Yes. Beautiful, with your blonde hair and blue eyes. He said it, and the mirror agrees.

They tell you about the child later. His child. Her child. Not your child.

"Poor thing, her mother is dead," they say.

You have them bring the child to you. She is quiet, small, and sweet. She is also lovely. At age seven, she makes grown men stutter when she enters a room. You smile at her and try to talk, but she does not want to talk. Her dark eyes stare accusation at you from her pale face. You are in her mother's place.

She does not like that.

She does not like you.

You send her away. Back to her nurse, back to her games, back to whatever it is that she does, in her silent beauty. You wish that you could like her, that you could be friends, but when you think of calling her back, you remember her eyes and the way she tossed her black hair—darker than midnight in a graveyard—when she left. You decide that you need not contend with the child. She does not want to talk to you. You can accept that.

After all, you are not her mother.

"There is no heir," he says to you. The mirror reflects the glittering gaze of his crown. He wears it always. When he wooed and won you, you did not think that you were marrying a man who would wear his crown to visit you.

You smile in the mirror, into your beautiful face over his shoulder, and you consider saying: There is the girl. And then you remember her lips, scarlet and smiling a tiny, secret smile as you pass her in the halls.

Looking back at his eyes, you say, "I will see the midwife."

She gives you a potion to drink. It will increase your fertility, she says. Hatred oozes from her small dark eyes. You wonder whether she tells you truth or whether the black bottle is poison, but you smile at her—at yourself in the mirror as you look past her impassive face and vicious eyes—and thank her. You are to drink the potion thrice daily, she says, and holds out her filthy, grasping hand for the payment.

In time, you are able to advise him that you are with child. He nods carelessly and pats your head in precisely the same way he pets his favorite hound bitch. Days pass. He does not come to you to perform that act in the middle of the night that you pretend to loathe and secretly crave.

Mirror, mirror...

The mirror shows your high, round breasts above the stays that press into your skin so deeply that you sometimes bleed at night. They keep your waist so narrow that his hands can span it and often have, but not now, not through the changes of the moon from new to quarter to half. Tomorrow night the moon will be full. If you are beautiful, why will he not come to you? Was this all that he wanted from you, for you to sweat and scream and bleed until an heir slides from between your thighs?

Why does he absent himself?

A shimmer, a change, and the mirror answers. You see yourself far gone with child, your belly bulging out in front of you like a millstone attached to your body. Your eyes are still blue, but they are tired, and deep, bruised shadows lurk under them. Your blonde hair is limp and unwashed. A cheap cotton dress hangs on your frame, strained across the breasts and stomach. The image repulses you, and you shove it away, realizing what you do only when your hands touch the mirror.

The image vanishes, replaced by you as you are now.

When you are vomiting and the blood is running down your thighs, you look into the mirror, over the shoulder of the maids. As they wail and cry for the loss of his heir, the mirror shows you the image again of yourself, heavy and tired. The image gradually shrinks and brightens until you see yourself: not the woman huddled over a basin with a rag clutched to her pelvis, but the true you. The beautiful you.

Between the heaves, you smile a tiny, secret smile.

The second time you paid the midwife, the money was better spent.

"I will never betray you, my lady. Never." She lied, but you knew that as you watched her eyes shift in the mirror. No matter. You had planned for that, remembering the sour turn of her mouth and the way she stared at you from the corners of her eyes. You are the queen. Treachery is treason and treason is punishable by death.

On the wall...

He would not come to you in the night, but another would.

Another did.

Beauty is power. You thought it was all the power that a woman could have until you discovered what men would do for a few short minutes of being sheathed inside you.

The mirror shows your breasts hanging down as the huntsman plunges into you, ecstasy and agony one in his face. For a moment, he is beautiful, as you look at his reflection. Then your view clears and you see that he is but a man, rutting as men do. He tells you that he loves you, over and over, as he kisses your pink mouth and the curve of your hip and the arch of your foot. Then he goes, and once he is gone, you wash quickly and thoroughly.

Staring into the mirror, you think of his words and you wonder: what is love?

Perhaps he will come soon. He intends to get you with child again. How long will it take until he realizes that it will not happen? Until he no longer comes to your room with its tapestries and the clinging scent of your perfume?

No matter.

That feeling, the small shameful warm feeling, that you used to have in your bed with him at night, it is gone. It may have left the first time with the huntsman, or perhaps it was when you swallowed the midwife's potion. You wash male scent from your skin, and you think that perhaps you imagined that feeling before.

You never felt anything during the act.

How could you have?

No, nothing.

A knock sounds at the door, and when you stand to open it, the mirror shows your beauty.

The perfect porcelain skin that you had when you came eight years ago is no longer so perfect. From a distance, you are the same, but the mirror shows your truth. The mirror shows your age: twenty-six. You see the fine, fine lines around your eyes. The mirror shows the thickening of your waist, and your breasts are no longer so round and high. A faint shadow under your jaw causes you to look more closely, and it is then that you see it. Sagging flesh, there, under your chin.

You are appalled, and a sneaking terror twists its way into your soul.

Who is...

You are the fairest, the mirror says. You nod, and when you wave away the food that they bring you, when you are doubled up in bed from the cramps of your belly, when your ribs bleed and ache from the tightening of the corset, you remember. The fairest of them all. So you are. So you must remain.

As the huntsman bends you over, you fix your eyes on the mirror.

You are twenty-eight.

"Beautiful, my lady, she is the most beautiful girl I have ever seen," says the huntsman as he toys with your hair.

Girl.

You are no longer a girl. There is a sudden sharp pain, and you wince. He has pinched you, roughly. The hands that once handled you with care and awe are different now. They know that you cannot object, that in the death that lies between you is the power, for he understands—he has always understood—why the midwife had to die. For a short time, he was yours.

Now, you are his.

Beauty and sex and power.

What do you have?

When the huntsman goes, you dally before washing. The other has not come to your chamber for sixteen moons. Some girl. She must be from the village, they say, whispering as they bustle about your chamber, pretending that they do not know you can hear. Some girl. You wonder if he wears his crown when he visits her.

The fairest...

When you ask, the mirror shows you the girl. Hair black as a moonless eve, lips red as blood.

You have nothing.

"Do you understand?"

He nods with no hesitation. "Kill the girl."

"Take her to the forest first," you correct sharply. No one may know, no one may hear, and most of all, no one may see. Only you will see, if the mirror chooses to show you. The huntsman's eyes glitter in the mirror. They shift, like the eyes of the midwife.

To your surprise, it hurts.

The mirror chooses to show you.

Of them...

As you watch him take his pleasure of her—a payment she completes with alacrity, suggesting that perhaps she is not so sweet as she seemed, and with an enthusiasm that makes you think of a small, warm feeling you might have had once—before sending her off into the forest, your chest hurts. A sharp, painful stab, almost as though someone has plunged a knife into your heart. You carefully apply the paint to your too-pale cheeks, and the feeling fades.

When he comes back, his eyes go to your cheeks, with their artificial color.

In the mirror, you see pity in his face. Looking away, you offer him the mulled wine: warmth against the cold of the forest he so recently entered. He takes it, and then he takes you, and this time, you do not watch in the mirror.

As he lies on the funeral bier, you smile a small, secret smile.

Treachery is treason.

Moons pass while you plan. The mirror shows you the girl, surrounded by the small, hairy men of the forest. She lives with them, paying them as she paid the huntsman. But sometimes, they must leave. To gather food. To hunt. One day, when they go hunting, so do you.

She is pathetically grateful to see you, and the fear that she might recognize you passes within moments. After all, it has been ten years since she tossed her hair as she left your rooms, ten years since her dark eyes measured you and found you wanting. Now she smiles, talks endlessly as she has you sit near the fire: "Here, Mother, warm yourself at the hearth."

Mother.

You are ten years older than she, ten only. The warmth that you had begun to feel at her artless chatter dissipates. She accepts your gift with the same enthusiasm she gave to the huntsman—your huntsman—and you watch as she greedily eats the sweet.

"It comes from the castle, my lady," you say to her. "My cousin gave it to me."

She does not ask why you have chosen to give it to her, just as she did not question your presence. Instead, she licks the crumbs from her fingers and smiles, satisfied. She does not say thank you. No thanks are necessary for what she expects as her due. She is beautiful.

All.

When she chokes, her hands going to her throat, you watch until she lies on the floor, her black hair pooling around her, her red lips a stark contrast to the paleness of her skin—skin white as death. Then you pick up your basket and you turn to leave, but you go to her and close her dark, staring eyes.

Why did she call you "Mother"?

Perhaps you always knew that there was no hope, that one day she would come back. One day is sooner than you expected, but in a way, it is a relief. The mirror shows you her return, triumphant as the foreign prince holds her before him on his steed. You watch until they are only a few leagues from the palace, until the mirror shows you her face. She is twenty, now. Six years until she, too, begins to fade.

Fewer if she becomes a mother.

Before you step out of the window, you open the carved cherry-wood doors of the mirror and gaze into it. You consider breaking the mirror. Saving her. She has done nothing, except take that which the world allows her to have—a small portion, soon to be lost, just as yours has been.

She called you "Mother."

Perhaps the cycle could change.

Then the doors swing closed, protecting the mirror. Try as you might, you cannot open them.

"She is dead, my lady," they say. "Stepped right out of the window, we don't know why she would have done it." They look out of the window, down at her body lying broken and still on the pavement, and they shake their heads. "So beautiful, she was, too. So very beautiful."

When they go, you open the carved cherry-wood shutters and gaze into the mirror. The corset squeezes your lungs as it compresses your waist, and the weight of the gown he gave you is exhausting. But they make you beautiful.

Beautiful?

Mirror, mirror, on the wall

Who is the fairest of them all?

You are, I say.

Yes. Beautiful, with your black hair and your red lips. I agree.

For now.

This is how we begin.

The Need To Stay the Same

Jo Walton

The Need To Stay the Same, by Si.
A review by Dorui.

The Need to Stay the Same is the latest of Si's "humans" sequence, and at eight offerings so far the world and themes are starting to feel familiar.

This is the story of a human called Bruce who comes to the city of Quingale on the cusp of Autumn. Bruce, like all Si's heroines, is an outsider with a problem. Bruce's particular and specific problem is different from those in the earlier stories—what it is and how it works out is a lot of why this is in the end worth your time, and I don't want to spoil it for you. But beyond the particulars of who Bruce is and what kind of transformation it is that has brought her to Quingale, this is something we've seen before.

In a world where humans now have a kaleidoscopic variety of options as far as gender, sexuality and bodies go, they are still bound to the physical, they still have to live in bodies. That's the joy and horror of the series, of course, the very physicality of the characters—they eat, they make love, they move from place to place all in the physical world. Si is as good as ever at describing the sensations of humanity— the changes in temperature, the tastes, the scents, even touch, the hardest to imagine of all. There's a stunning sequence here where Bruce longs to scratch her nose but is prevented by social convention, which really made me believe what it would be like to have a nose and an itch.

But while this use of physicality was revolutionary and astonishing in the justly celebrated *Birth and Death*, and still exciting and fascinating in subsequent volumes, I'm getting a little tired of it. Yes, Bruce's body makes an involuntary twitch as she shivers in a cold wind—I remember the same thing happening to Lu Song in *Living Without You*. Sure, the leaves that have helped trees convert sunlight to nutrients all summer are slowly drifting to the ground, and yes, it's an amazing piece of chemical and biological imagination, but it was described in *The Flowers In The Wheelbarrow*. It's interesting that now the fixed genders of earlier books have ceased to be a problem, but I never really cared about that anyway. And clever as it all is, you have to admit it's a long way removed from real life.

Si's genius is in making these "humans", so different from us, so like us in some essential ways. I'm not a huge fan of the explanations of Si's weirder inventions like "photosynthesis" and "orgasm", but I do appreciate the level at which emotion is universal. There were ways in which I could identify with Bruce, in her ever changing quest for stability. Inter-personal relationships are one of Si's true strengths, and I really do feel after reading this that it doesn't matter if it's bodies under a sheet with heat and touch and secretions, or minds longing for merger—we reach out to each other in the same ways. Bruce's impediment is not the same kind of impediment as those we suffer, but it still has emotional resonance, and I cared. I wanted Bruce to find fulfillment, even the strange kind of fulfillment that's what's available for humanity.

Still, in the end, eight of anything is surely enough? We've been paying attention to these "humans" for a long time, it must be hours now. This is a good addition to the series, it's powerful, and Si does manage to pull some surprises here and there. But I think it's time for a new series, for Si's wild invention to bring us something else, something with characters just this great, and ideas just as alien as the concept of physical flesh, but new.

Bottom Drawer

Brett Savory

In my office is a desk.

My desk contains three drawers, each slightly bigger than the one above it. The top drawer is where I keep my stationery; the middle drawer contains mainly instruction manuals for my computer, a scientific calculator, and other devices; and the bottom drawer is where I hide things.

Four years ago, when job stress got to be too much, I hid a bottle of whiskey in this bottom drawer. Hid it, but never touched it. It's still there, unopened, pushed to the back. After that, I hid a handgun. It's loaded, sitting next to the whiskey, unused now for three years.

This worked for a little while, made things easier, knowing that when depression hit, I had some whiskey and a gun. I could take action.

If I wanted to.

But for the past year, it hasn't been enough, and I've realized that this stress has little to do with my job. I feel ashamed when I think of the whiskey bottle and the gun, because I know I'd never use them.

A few months ago, I started hiding receipts for mundane things, like movie tickets, wiper blades, bags of chips, DVDs, everything.

Until last week, when I decided to use my bottom drawer to hide more important things, things that *deserved* to be next to the whiskey bottle and the gun.

In a tiny envelope, beside the bottle, I carefully placed my dream that I'd find someone to share my life with. In another envelope, I breathed my sexual secrets, licked the glue along the envelope's flap, tucked it snugly under the gun.

I filled the middle of the drawer with pages of conversations written in longhand—discussions, as well as I can remember them, with people no longer in my life. I stapled these together, grouped by association.

Friend, parent, lover, child.

I wrapped my love for my children in elastic bands, left it near the front of the drawer, so I could find it easily. So that on very bad days, my hand would touch this knotted bundle before finding the items at the back.

At night, when people drifted lazily out the doors to their successful lives, I locked my top two drawers, but always left the bottom drawer unlocked—and slightly open, maybe a quarter of an inch.

I wanted someone to open it. A nosy cleaning lady. A curious co-worker. Maybe they'd be inspired to add things of their own, wrap little pieces of their lives in stationery, nestle them next to my secrets. Hiding who they really were, who they really wanted to be, just to make life easier.

But every morning, I'd come into the office, and no one had opened it; no one had touched a thing.

Last night, after work, I opened my bottom drawer, leaned over and pushed down with both hands, shoved it all as far back as possible.

Let them try now. Let them work for it. Let them sweat. Courage takes work.

Liquid Loyalty Ten Years On
(poem)

Sequel to "Liquid Loyalty" in *TFF* 26 (2013)

Redfern Jon Barrett

Anya never lost Rachel.
No, that isn't true. There were times she forgot, when she was wrapped in other lovers,
in young arms,
and firm breasts.
Few at first,
then more.
And now they lived, perched cliff-high, a ragged house, a ragged people. Torn from Loyalty's bliss, left with only one another, with the ocean far below.

Anya never lost Rachel.
The library woman burst into thought
every day,
near every day.
(Often at first,
then less so.)
She danced atop memories.
And she'd have been welcomed, open-armed and open-hearted. Embraced by a group of misfits, perched at the edge of the world.

Anya never lost Rachel.
Though she'd waited,
and though she'd waited,
every day,
almost every day.
But then came Lucy,
and Bryan,
and Charles.
And she'd stroll the streets, searching for others with clear eyes and open minds, looking for Rachel. Always looking for Rachel.

Anya never lost Rachel,
she never lost anything,
it was all there still.
Bus drivers
and poster people
and invisible vandals
and empty-gazed colleagues.

The lover;
her husband.
And yes, he was there too, in her scattered recollection, in that rickety
house above the sea. Her husband, lost in Liquid, ever-pining, never-
ending.

Anya never lost Rachel,
And she never found her either,
and it broke her heart,
and it drove her on,
ever on,
and she never stopped thinking,
of the smell of books,
and of history-dust,
and of the library woman,
deep underground.
And yes she was happy, and yes she hoped, she knew, that the house
was the seed which could spring the world anew. And while they piled
with one another, while all around were bellies and birthmarks, flashes
of white and pink and brown and orange, there among the bodies she
would see Rachel. Never lost, ever lost, a woman and a memory, both
she'd love forever, both who'd set her free.

Always Look on the Bright Side

Alison Littlewood

In summer of 2008, with the help of Peter Tennant, TFF ran a writing contest. Entrants were challenged to produce a work of writing of less than 1000 words, creatively incorporating at least four of the following phrases, all of which were taken from the subject lines of spam e-mail:

— *Transform into a sex god*
— *Being small is a crime*
— *Hit your home run today*
— *Get huge, get large, get our pills*
— *Free starter pack changes my life*
— *Be every guy's envy*
— *She loves you more each day*
— *Happiness is not hard to obtain*
— *Never agree to be a loser*
— *Monstrous results today*

Alison's was the winning story, voted by the attendees of the 2008 Whisper-and-Fire Con.

Bugger it. I wonder what Daniel Craig would have done. Probably waggled his little finger and they'd have all been swooning, falling at his feet or something. Wish I could do that. Transform into a sex god. Be every guy's envy. Happiness is not hard to obtain when you're six foot tall and built like the brick proverbial. Wonder if he was ever sick on someone's shoes. Nope: didn't think so.

It was all down to my mate Zach. He gave me this pep talk. "It's not what you say, Kevin, it's how you say it. In life, you have to think big. Being small is a crime, in business as in love. Never agree to be a loser. Think loud, think proud, think the world is your oyster. Imagine you live at the Savoy, drive a Zonda, have Kylie begging for it, like she loves you more each day. You know she would, if she could. Grab life by the balls, Kev."

He calls me Kev, I think he thinks it's jaunty. I call him a tosser, but not to his face. Still, you can't be choosy when you have no money, no woman and no friends. Everyone else I knew had gone to uni. Zach just never seemed to want to leave, and I'd failed to get in.

"Get a life," said Zach, as though they had them on shelves at the supermarket. "Get out there. Get a proper job. Get a girl. Get up and get going. Get something, for God's sake. Get huge, get large, get our pills."

"What?" I said.

"Well, maybe not pills," he said. "I'm not sure you're quite ready for that stage in your development. They're for the bold, you know. For the brave. Although it worked for me." He tapped a finger against his nose, as though he knew something I didn't. "Free starter pack changes my life. That's what they all say. Guaranteed."

"What sort of pills?"

"Oh, you know. Few 'erbs. Spices. Spice up your life." He pulled a little package out of his pocket. They didn't have a label. He put them into my hands and leaned in, confidentially. "Hit your home run today," he said.

I took one just before work. My first day it was, on the shop floor, and a big grin spread across my face soon as I walked in. I whistled this tune under my breath, 'Always look on the bright side of life', and I did. For me, the sun was shining, everything was beautiful, and I could dance like Fred Astaire. So I did, right down the electrical aisle, and into the arms of my new boss. I grabbed her by the waist, spun her round, and told her it was good to be alive.

"Are you quite all right, Kevin?" she asked. "Only you're supposed to be sweeping the floor down in canned goods. There's a baby been sick in aisle three."

"I," I said, quite slowly, "am not a floor sweeper of life. Am not a floor sweeper of anything, in fact. Born to better things. And you, may I say, are too. You're looking quite gorgeous. Sexier than Kylie Minogue's arse." I fell to one knee, grabbed something off the shelf and held it out to her. In my head, it was a red, red rose. In fact, it was the new Nokia 4630i, 30% off.

She stared at it. "You're fired," she said, precisely seven minutes after I'd walked in.

That was when I was sick on her shoes.

"Get a life," Zach had said. "Get a job. Get a girl." Yeah, right. Bollocks. Get fired, get humiliated, get sick. Get gone. Monstrous results today.

Then I looked at my boss' lips, all pursed up like a cat's behind, and the trainees, their mouths hanging open, and wondered.

Free starter pack changes my life? Well, I suppose it did. Can't complain. Never agree to be a loser, that's what he said.

Transform into a sex god. Be every guy's envy. Happiness is not hard to obtain. And I started to whistle…

Mermaid Teeth, Witch-Honed

Benjanun Sriduangkaew

Where you come from, the world is no color at all and the cold is hadopelagic.

Like anything of the deep, you're born from bulbous translucent eggs, your gaze open and aware in utero, learning marching orders even before she breaks the membrane of your birth and pulls you out by the hand. This is your first touch, your first understanding of tactility: her webbed fingers tapering to knifepoints, her deep-set eyes cupped in scales, whiteless.

You tear open the weakest of your sisters, and that is your first food, your first understanding of hunger and devouring and savoring: their hearts like fists, their innards like pearls, their bottomless ichor feeding your arteries. Their teeth and fingers anoint you with your first scars.

When the feeding is done you are lined up with other sibling-victors, each of whom has been brought forth the same: skin just so, a nose like this, irises perfect and lashes beguiling—they are not characteristics that will help in surviving the clutching hooks and tails of the depths. You have been made for another purpose, sculpted to specifications of a different world. Still you are not weak; she will allow no fragility. Underneath you are more than gristle and fat. Your face and form hide the absolute certainty of the abyss.

The world above, she has been whispering through your eggs, is full of light and riches, and its people very soft. Their hides do not withstand the tides; their mouths may not draw life from the salt, and their hearts crush easily under the claws of the waves. They are food for the sharks and the eelish whips that inhabit the ground of this city, the ground of your birth-chamber. But a day will arrive when above and below become one, and you are to prepare the path.

The witch is not your mother and you are not her child. She is your instructor and you are her cadet. This is how it works, a foundation, a transaction. Success is currency. Elevation is the ultimate good, and conquest is written into your marrow.

Here is a pair of legs. You will not walk on it as if on broken glass, though it will be hard at first. But you have known harder, and your muscles are better than steel, born and shaped to the cold and its unrelenting grip, its resistance to passage.

Here is a voice for the land above. You will not be mute, though it will be hard at first. But in the breeding chamber you have known harder, and your throat may produce any noise, born and shaped to the calls of the deep, the equal of any predators and the darkling pits that spit terrors.

Here is armor for your limbs. Here is an ear for language. Here is a box of metamorphosis, a secret to eternity, and nine eel-charms to proof you against the scorching sun. They are your sidearm.

The way up is not easy, but you are among the best of a brood molded for strength and speed. You will allow no failure.

You are discipline and might and will. March.

Making shore you cannot walk, but you crawl and push, striving against unfamiliar air, unfamiliar dry. The charms live just next to your bones, coiling alive inside your ribcage; that way they may not be seen or heard or stolen from you. In the human languages there are more words for theft than the abyssal tongues have for ocean, though you do have precise vocabulary for many kinds of killing: sorted according to the method, circumstance and motive. But as a species, a realm, you have no need to rob. Everything knows its place, in the structure of rank and hierarchy, the intricate chain of food and devourer. Order of birth, puissance of sinew, length of teeth and measure of heritage: those are destiny.

Salt shines on your lips, rattling in your mouth unmelting like loose teeth.

This is how they find you: a man, a woman. Old and sun-withered, their ankles scarred by the fangs of fish, their hands scourged by nets and ropes. Their hides are rougher and tougher than you were given to expect, and their hair snags in the wind desiccated and white. They lead you to their home.

In parts of the world above they believe eating mermaid flesh will extend life, restore youth. You are not the mermaid of their scripts and spoken tales; you are the image and your flesh is poison. Still you will not allow them to taste—to permit that is to forfeit your place. Predator or prey. To be one is to deny the other, permanently. That is the verity encrypted into the deep, the same code that rules existence even here, though those of the dry do not yet know it.

In a way, your task is in part to educate.

You are ready when they come with gutting knives. It is night, but your sight has been made for much darker. The knives are sharp, but your teeth are sharper still. This is no challenge. Somewhere there must be a tale of meeting in peace and family-making across species, but that is not one of yours.

You try their meat, but it is lean and troubled with too many years of bad living, of sickness; you spit most of it out. Their clothes become yours, tatters foreign against your sea-hide. Their food goes to feed you and the eels.

The air parches and the day scorches; the threshing depths call.

Locomotion comes to you, step by step, a battle waged by your ligaments on this harsh thin air, this emptiness of being. The theater is your own body, your own gravity, this world's lack of buoyancy— mass distributes differently, there is no current to push and pull. At first you are beaten, must retreat to the shadow to rest stressed calves and knees not used to either existing or bipedalism. You sip the sea-smells for sustenance, and if you do not know affection for your sisters, still you are capable of feeling their absence like a missing finger, a missing fin.

Your duels progress, and in time you win the match more often than you lose. You are upright, most hours, on two feet. Attrition plays in your favor and your stamina, so close to shore, is extensive. This would be different further on, or in a desert, or up the mountains where the witch's voice may not reach. But she has chosen a battlefield to your advantage and hers.

The prince and his entourage arrive, appointment-exact, true to her predictions. His fascination in you is immediate, and he takes a strand of your hair, marvels at its darkness that seems to drink light. Marvels at the dew on your shoulders like black rain that never dries, and he calls you a princess of the waves. He takes your hand, limned in shivering blue-green, and raises it to his lips. His mouth is warm, and interests you as a morsel of food might. There is enough of him to make several meals, once you peel the trappings away to find the lymph underneath, the arterial brilliance, the cardiac delight. You imagine them this way: perfectly indented to your incisors, perfectly textured to your molars.

His gaze follows your face the way prey follows the lure of an anglerfish. He asks a question. His speech is not yet yours to master, but he takes silence as *yes*. In dry-language there are many words for no, but they ascribe barely any meaning to it. *No* signifies nothing. There is only yes. So when the time comes you will not ask, because they have already given assent. Yes to the sea, yes to mermaids, yes to their correct place under the rule of the deep.

His kingdom is, of course, itself near sea: cliff-faced, tide-lashed. A good strategist takes into account every phase of combat, and the witch is very good. Site selection and terrain are among the foremost concerns.

Here is a string of gold and diamonds. Here is a comb of ivory and serving-girls to use it on your serpent-hair. Here is a gift, a gift, a gift. They are your spoils of war, surrendered in advance.

The witch is your general and you are her infantry. Advance.

Palace rooms and palace halls, tapestries and gilded paintings in their frames of stone. Bed and bridal drapes, crowns and scepters in their caskets of rule. Silverware and ceramic, fluted glasses filled to the brim with juices drawn from the soil. These are the grammar of otherness.

They line your bed with muslin and your waist with rose-gold, circle your throat in emeralds and burden your earlobes with nacre. Even your feet are not allowed to meet the ground bare: it must first be sheathed in velvet and beaded with pearls. You like pearls; they are mined from injury, and if they aren't from home—too shallow—pearls are still closer kin to you than the maids, the prince, his courtiers. Mirrors may suggest otherwise, but only those of the land trust in mirrors. They look at nose, mouth, shape and color of eyes. They search the jawline, the angle of cheeks. They do not peer inside to measure the keenness of your teeth, to question the arrangement of the cords in your throat, to examine the operation of your lungs and larynx. They do not admit the possibility that the outward form is malleable.

The maids do notice that you smell ever of salt, but they are trained to politeness and quiet, to be seen and not heard. They steer you onto the path to being much the same, and that is no ordeal, for what have you to say to them? Your ears are primed to the witch's mandates. The rest is noise. Turquoise and blue sapphires are what they like best on you, at brow and neck and wrist, calling them the hues of the waves even though your point of origin denies color. No filigree netting is risked on your hair, which never dries. Pillowcases are rotated rapid-fire, tablecloths replaced after each meal.

In the meanwhile you practice music. The prince loves to hear you sing.

Mermaid song is knives, is scalpels. It bypasses the more patient process of fleshly impetus, the ungainliness of mating between deep-kind and dry-kind. It sculpts and molds. Your notes infiltrate the stems of spine, the gaps between vertebrae, the synaptic interstices between the constituents of the brain. Your music embeds under gums and latches onto diaphragm and the lining of stomachs. Even the liver and pancreas must alter; no component may be left untouched.

Mermaid teeth are stronger than anything. You could make food of the jewels they pour into your lap, but there's no savor to the taste. Up here you have acquired a liking for warm raw meat, the deceptive softness of it, the pungent wealth in each bite. Of all land-things it is not the perfume or the silk that has captivated you—the sweet heat of meat is by far the better offering, and you think your sisters will like this too. Some of them are at work elsewhere, witch-hatched and witch-honed to a single purpose. But you are determined to be the best.

You master your melodies, capture them in beads of hematite and agate, and give them to servants. Learn to laugh for them: a gift, a gift, a gift. Your song is carried from house to house, and if each bead doesn't fetch much at market, still it is something. It's more than they have ever been given from the court, which tends to pass them no better than the dregs of a meal and the tatters of a dress. They thank you, love you for your charity, the essential virtue of a land-maiden along with beauty and music sweeter than their gods.

You listen and you watch, studying. But unless pressed for words, you keep your silence, save for song. Your voice is tuned just so, precious as rose-gold sashes, and they come for it, line up to hear your notes transmute the alchemy of their lymph, their veins, the inner mechanisms of their bodies. Each refrain brings them a step closer to kinship. The effect will be slow and their hearts will not rupture suddenly, nor their bones shift in your presence, for you understand danger. Mermaid skin is hard but it can be punctured; the witch made you well but her composition will not save you from a blade between your ribs. You will not survive the stone wheels through which they put their enemies, their heretics, their prisoners. So went the fisherman, first to screams, then to smears of fat and gore.

Humans from other nations will wonder, afterward. They will tell each other little lies of a wicked creature from deep below, spurned by a human prince with shining hair and sapphire eyes or else jealous of a human princess with skin like snow. They will say the witch was angered that men of the dry will not have her. Stories proliferate like the bloom of anemones.

Your instructor and general is not interested in such; she is above them, beyond the reach of their stories. The truth is otherwise. It is the nature of predators to hunger and expand. As the arrow of time moves only in one direction, so does the witch: her course is inexorable and the fabric of being makes way. And thus, your sisters. And thus, you.

They fit you for a crown, a gown, a scepter. They select the bridal flowers for you to grip, the vast train of your skirts, the children who will hold them above the dirt and stained flagstones.

Will you marry him? Will you become his queen? Will you sit on this throne? You give the silence that says *of course* but it's not as though they would have interpreted your sealed lips and still tongue for anything else.

At the ceremony you will ride through the city, garlanded and jeweled, singing all the while. A voice that carries from bead to bead, roof to roof, reverberating in cobblestones and between walls.

On the night of your nuptial, your army mobilizes. You know the exact instant at which each cobbler and potter, each trader and laborer, turns. Hair sheds and ears sink back into the skull, flesh turns to sea-hide and scales. Pupils to sclera, and thought of land to thought of tide. Blood to ichor.

They cry out in the streets as it happens, their insides twisting and shaping to adjust for the coming change. It is not painless.

In the wedding chamber, the prince curls in on himself. Coils of his hair fall free from his skull, strewn like dead eels. The metamorphosis was meant to be much more ponderous, stretching across a frame of decades. Accelerated to several days, truncated to a few hours, it is agony. For him, and for the rest, there is room for *before*—but when the process completes, they will have to learn to put *before* aside. They will thank you.

When the witch comes, she brings the sea. It roars before her and lifts her up, her chariot of tides.

In the language of the deep there are many words for desire and delight; you whisper them now in the witch's ear as you take her into your arms. You lead her to a throne of masts made of pearl, sails made of silk and crowns. You show her the new brood that you have created with your voice.

In the language of mermaids there are no words for mercy. Predators do not show leniency to prey. The land above is a stomach cracked wide open. It is yours to fill, until all is ocean, until all is yours. The world entire will be the deep.

The witch is your queen and you are her commander.

Forward.

Sweet Like Fate

Sara Puls

Lambeth had no right to lurk in the shadows during Ru's solo practice time beneath the Big Top. An aerialist, Ru was the best performer the *Nouveau Cirque de Agua Dulce* had. No one else came close to rivaling her strength, her grace, her free fall drops. As for Lambeth, she was just the sideshow. The freak. The misfit. The weirdo. *Lambeth the Bearded Lady! See her beard! Watch her whiskers grow!*

Still, Lambeth couldn't help but be drawn to Ru. It wasn't the way Ru's body twisted and gyrated around the fabric. And it wasn't the way her muscles pulsed when she latched back onto the silks after a staggering drop. What made Ru so irresistible were the wyrds written on her skin.

Lambeth noticed the first wyrd after the troupe's performance in El Paso. In the chaotic shuffle back into the ring for a final bow, Lambeth stumbled into line behind Ru.

Still glistening from her performance—the last of the show—Ru wiped sweat from her brow. Her chest rose and fell in quick, oxygen-hungry breaths. Lambeth soaked in the acrobat's every move.

As the line of performers lurched forward, Ru lifted her hair with one hand and wiped down her neck with the other. That's when Lambeth saw it. Written in delicate, inky script across Ru's neck was the wyrd

breathe

Lambeth stepped closer but the wyrd faded away. Still, she knew what she saw. One moment flawless walnut skin, the next a secret wyrd. A wyrd meant for... whom?

As Ru let her dark curls fall back into place, Lambeth sized her up. She was smart. She was tall and thin, like a giraffe. She had big, bright eyes and skin that seemed to sparkle as she danced. She was strong, too. And until that moment she had seemed so—*normal.*

Lambeth heeded the wyrd and took a long, slow breath.

Suddenly the ringmaster—Master Fortune McLeroy —was calling out Ru's name.

Ladies and gentlemen! I give you the beautiful, the elegant, the incredible... Ru!

Crisp, cheerful applause erupted from the hands of each and every body in the crowd.

Lambeth was next. She straightened her skirt and smoothed her beard—which was really more of a goatee.

Lambeth, everyone! Lambeth the Bearded Lady. Give 'er a round of applause.

A few people whistled and clapped as Lambeth stepped forward. As she curtsied, though, the more typical remarks sliced through the thin, lazy applause.

Sick. Just sick.

Freak!

Feigning ignorance, Lambert straightened up, forced a smile, and waved—from the elbow, not the wrist.

As she stepped back into line, she turned her gaze towards Ru, who looked at her with strange, almost sad eyes. Just before Ru looked away, Lambeth saw another wyrd. This one, arched over Ru's left eyebrow, said

forget

Lambeth longed to pull Ru close for a better view. Instead, mind racing, unable to catch her breath, she turned back to the crowd.

The next performance, this time in Nuevo Laredo, passed by much like all the rest. With the grace of a swan, Ru contorted herself between the long lengths of fabric that hung from the ceiling. Marcel pranced across the tightrope with barely a wobble. One of the dancing elephants refused to dance. And Lambeth permitted a mixture of jeers and jabs to rain down on her from the crowd.

That's no woman! yelled a gruff voice from the stands.

Sure feel bad for her husband, another called.

A wave of laughter pushed across crowd.

Nah, she ain't got a man. Lookit her!

Lambeth knew she was far from beautiful. But this? She didn't deserve this.

Hey, lady, some kid yelled, disrupting her thoughts. *Let's see you give that ugly ol' beard a tug!*

Lambeth sighed through a beaming, painful smile and obliged the request. Fortune said it was important to prove her beard wasn't a fake. Most of them were.

As the crowd hooted and laughed, Lambeth finally made her escape. Ru stood partly behind the crushed velvet curtain that led backstage.

Ru's sympathetic half-smile took Lambeth by surprise. Despite their brief exchange in El Paso, she still expected Ru to look right through her, like most of the troupe did.

"Rough crowd," Lambeth managed.

"Ain't it always?" And then, in a swirl of dark ink, the wyrd

strength

danced down Ru's left arm.

Three wyrds on three occasions. But before Lambeth could speak, Ru hurriedly pulled on her warm-up jacket and slipped into the folds of the faded burgundy curtain.

Two days later, when back at home in Agua Dulce, Lambeth could think only of those wyrds. Impressed into her mind like sunspots, their implications and mysteries would not fade away.

Maybe it was loneliness that compelled Lambeth to sneak into the Big Top during Ru's practice time. Or maybe it was simply that those wyrds—*breathe, forget, strength*—were the closest thing to understanding she'd experienced since joining the *Nouveau Cirque de Agua Dulce* three months earlier. Maybe she had nothing to lose.

Whatever it was, by then the choice to reveal what she knew felt like the only choice there could be. Standing just behind the aging curtains, next to a dusty heap of elephants' dance shoes, she watched and waited for the right moment.

With each twist and stretch of Ru's body, the air, a willing supplicant to the acrobat's charm and power, parted and split, sparkled and glimmered. Like Ru, it moved and bent in ways Lambeth never knew possible.

Finally, Ru swooped down from the practice silks with the ease of a cat scaling down a tree. Then, with both feet planted firmly on the ground, she spoke.

"You don't have to hide," she called, voice rich and smooth like honey.

Crouching down, making herself small, Lambeth stepped further into the grey-black shadows.

"Lambeth," Ru called softly, "I know you're there."

Slowly, carefully, Lambeth stepped out from the dusty, backstage air.

Ru's face was relaxed, her eyes warm; not a single line of irritation marred her beauty. Lambeth inched forward as Ru moved towards her with quick, graceful steps.

Soon they stood together at the edge of the practice ring.

"What made you join?" Ru asked.

It was a good question. The *Nouveau Cirque de Agua Dulce* was not a *nouveau cirque* in any sense but name. All their equipment had been purchased at flea markets and yard sales in places like Sarasota, the Ringling Brothers' de facto company town. And despite all the complaints from elephant rights activists and camel equality groups, Fortune even insisted on keeping two dancing elephants and a talking camel in the ranks. Nothing *nouveau* about that. Poor things.

"What made me join?" Lambeth chortled. "Who knows?"

"Ha. Tell me about it," Ru said. "But really, I mean, what's in it for you?" Again her voice was gentle, careful.

Lambeth shook her head. If she spoke now, she'd definitely cry. She couldn't cry in front of Ru, strong and beautiful Ru. Trying to ignore the giant pit in her stomach, she blinked rapidly and wiped a bead of sweat from her brow.

"I, I don't know anymore," she finally said. "I thought things would be different." Then, quickly, she changed the subject. "Why did *you* join? Seems like you could have done anything."

Ru bit her lower lip. "No," she finally said. "I can't control it. The wyrds—I know you've seen them—they just come."

Lambeth blushed.

"When I feel strongly about something—positively, that is, happy—I can't stop them," Ru admitted. " I hate the circus, if you can believe it. And I hate aerial silks. But the gig keeps me safe. Or it did. Until you."

"What did I—"

Ru reached out and put a hand on Lambeth's shoulder. A warm glow illuminated the space beneath the worn red and white tent, making Ru look almost ethereal.

"Go ahead," she said. "Touch me. Here." She tapped lightly on her chest, just above the hem of her leotard. "You'll see."

"Oh no," Lambeth said. "I couldn't."

"Please."

As her stomach twisted into knots, Lambeth placed a shaky hand on Ru's chest. "How long should I wait?"

A tiny smile flickered on Ru's face. "You'll know."

A moment later a delicate burst of heat pulsed beneath Lambeth's hand. She pulled away.

The wyrd was

yes

"Yes?" Lambeth asked, wiping her palms on her shirt.

Ru's smile bloomed big and bright. "If I've been cold, I'm sorry. It's just, with the wyrds, I can't be too trusting. If the circus finds out they'd never let me leave. And I can't stay here forever."

Lambeth nodded.

"They can always get a new aerialist. But I doubt they could find another girl with little fates imprinted on her skin."

"Right," Lambeth stuttered. "Of course."

Playfully, Ru took Lambeth's hands in hers and squeezed. "I'm a freak, too," she laughed. "Whatever that means."

Ru hadn't said it like the others. There was no disdain or judgment in her voice. Finally, Lambeth allowed herself to relax.

Clearing her throat, Ru ran her hands down the sides of her leotard, as if trying to brush her nerves away. "So my answer is yes."

Now, with a rush of emotion, it clicked.

Slipping one are around Ru's waist, Lambeth leaned in. First, as her tongue grazed Ru's bottom lip, she tasted the perfect acceptance of the wyrd *yes*. Then, pressing hard against Ru's mouth, she tasted all the wyrds she'd been searching for. The taste was sweet—like fate.

An Unrecognized Masterwork

Bruce Boston

We have before us this week the first authorized translation of the long and long-acclaimed Portuguese masterpiece *Stamp Your Feet!* by Juan Luis Obregon. Although Obregon was a contemporary, and most likely an acquaintance, of such literary lions as Joyce, Hemingway, and Stein, he has remained in relative obscurity outside his native land. Until recently only two of Obregon's works have been available in English: the early pornographic love poem "Ode to a Thighchilada," and the puzzling yet often anthologized short story "Gherkin," a surreal tour de force that takes place entirely under brine and which Ford Maddox Ford accused of being "no more than a distended pickling recipe."

Like so many artistic figures of the Twentieth Century, Obregon lived in Paris throughout much of the 1920s. Yet early on he became known as a loner and eccentric, and seldom was he invited to the more influential salons. In one account he is described as "a small dark man with a fiendish chuckle who affected half a mustache, sometimes on the left side of his face, more often on the right." Another casts him as "barrel-chested, a fantastic drinker and womanizer, prone to unreasoning fits of temper." This last point is substantiated by Paris Police reports for 1927. In April of that year Obregon was arrested on the banks of the Seine while trying to drown a rag picker who had insulted his necktie.

Oddly enough, Obregon's only publications during this time were not as a creative writer, but as a critic for the short-lived art weekly *Le Bidet Bouillonne Partout*, where he was best remembered for his classic pronouncement, "*Dada... c'est caca!*" which earned him more than a few enemies and once again showed his tendency to swim against prevailing currents.

By 1930 the bubble had burst, the axe had fallen, the pigeons had come home to roost... in short, the Great Depression was in full swing and most expatriates had repatriated, some, such as Hemingway, returning home to increasing fame and fortune. This was not to be the case for Obregon. Portugal remained a relatively backward country, in large part illiterate. Although "Gherkin" and the apparently untranslatable "Stuffed Chile" had already established his reputation among a select coterie of his fellow literati, financial support was not forthcoming. Obregon wandered the streets of Lisbon, destitute and in increasingly poor health. Finally he was forced to take a job as a coat tree in a local tavern.

Despite such difficulties, indications are that the writer was mellowing with age. His moustache was now complete and in his only surviving letter, written to his mother, he states: "At last I have found gainful employment, and although it may be below what I consider my just station in life, at least I am serving my fellow man. Send me some paella, if you please."

Obregon's new calling was to be a brief one. In March of 1934, only a few weeks after the final pages of *Stamp Your Feet!* had been penned, a premature spring struck the streets of Lisbon. In the space of one afternoon the weather turned unseasonably warm, and Obregon, still loyally at his post, was suffocated by an abandoned overcoat. Yet his masterpiece lives on.

Like so many great novels of the twentieth century—*Ulysses, Gravity's Rainbow, Bushwacker's Reprise*—the central obsession of *Stamp Your Feet!* is with the nature of time. Time to go to work. Time for dinner. Time to go to bed. Time to get up in the morning. We follow the protagonist, Manual Emanual, through twenty-seven and a half days of his life as a bricklayer building public lavatories for a soccer stadium on the outskirts of Madrid. The fact that Obregon had never been to Madrid is further testimony to the range of his vision. As each brick is laid in place a whole new reality, both internal and external, unfolds before us.

In the first section of the book, Obregon amply demonstrates why in some quarters he has earned the appellation "Master of the Gerundive."

"...carrying the trowel, laying the mortar, taking a smoke, eating a box lunch, taking a smoke, riding the trolley, spitting in the street, avoiding the irate landlady, paying the gas bill, killing a cockroach, masturbating, going to sleep..."

And so it goes, page upon page, chapter after chapter, of accelerating verbal pyrotechnics, until in the closing scene of Part One, Manual is struck upon the head by an improperly secured washbasin and lapses into a coma for the remainder of the narrative.

In Part Two, Obregon evolved a new and radical literary form to portray the comatose state, a form later dubbed "stream of unconsciousness." Note that this preceded the publication of *Ulysses* and was a good thirty years before William Burroughs' so-called discovery of the cut-up method. Shredding fourteen newspapers with his bare hands, and covering himself with flour and water, Obregon rolled about on the floor, placing words upon the page in the same order in which they stuck to his body. The result, needless to say, is more than flat bread. Yet you must dive into this immense and sometimes disturbing novel for yourself if you hope to truly sample its flavor.

Though the translation leaves something to be desired, at times slipping back into Portuguese, we recommend *Stamp Your Feet!* to serious students of twentieth century literature and all inveterate insomniacs.

Published clothbound by Callipygian Press, 743 pages, $34.95. Paperback rights are up for grabs. Yet as Obregon himself warns us in "Ode to a Thighchilada"—"Don't you go grabbing/ more than you can swallow."

Je me souviens

Su J. Sokol

There are nine police cars. I count them again just to be sure and because counting usually calms me.

Arielle watches to see if I'm freaking out. I smile but she's not reassured. She reaches up to place her hand on my shoulder, asks if I want to leave. I tell her I'm OK. She's still concerned so I try a sexy smile this time. If she would kiss me now, I'd have somewhere pleasant to channel my beating heart. She leans towards me and I see that she's used her superpowers to read my mind again, but then another police car arrives, drawing her attention away.

Now ten police cars face two hundred and thirty-six demonstrators. We are peaceful, banging pots and chanting slogans. Our numbers include children, old people, commuters on bikes, dogs wearing red bandanas. A cop is speaking through a bullhorn but no one can hear him because of the clanging and chanting. Will they arrest us now? My heart beats like the wings of a falcon, trying to escape the prison of my chest.

I tell myself that this is Québec. They will not put a black bag over my head. They will not throw me in the trunk of one of their cars. They will not burn me with cigarettes after beating me. No, this doesn't happen here... I am pretty sure. They have granted me permanent residence and have even hired me to teach their children math. So I will stay here and demonstrate for my students.

The police open the trunks of their vans. I'm concentrating on my breathing, on not blanking out, when a little ball of energy in a red cape flies into my legs.

"*La policía*, they are here to catch the bad guys, Papa?" he asks me, his speech the usual jumble of French, Spanish and English.

Before I can speak, Arielle answers. "No, *mon petit chéri*, this is not why they're here today."

"*I* will catch them, then! But first Papa must fly me home so I can eat my supper."

"*C'est correct?* Can we go home now?" Arielle asks me.

I shrug, hiding my relief, and lift Raphaël high over my head. I run full out towards our home, fast enough so that his cape flies out behind him and fast enough that my own need to run is satisfied. Our four-year-old superhero has come to the rescue.

The next morning, despite a sleep fragmented by nightmares, I'm energized, thinking about being a part of something important again. This was not my first demonstration in my new home, but the first of *this* kind—spontaneous, focused, a little confrontational. And joyous. Even more so than the mass *manifestation* when our numbers first surpassed 250,000.

That day, I stood at the overpass by rue Berri, Raphaël on my shoulders, watching the street below swell with a current of demonstrators wide as the Rio Grande. I'm good at counting, my eyes instinctively grouping people into hundreds, thousands, tens and hundreds of thousands. Surely they must listen now, I thought. Surely they will see the beauty, the rightness of our cause!

Our euphoria was short-lived as we watched the news and listened to the lies about our goals, our numbers. Last night, with our pots, with our "casseroles", we banged out our anger and turned it into music. We felt our connection to the other Montréal *quartiers* out in the street from Parc Ex to Pointe-Saint-Charles, Snowdon to St. Michel to Villeray to Verdun. I am proud, too, that *les casseroles*, "los caserolazos", are borrowed from the political traditions of my own people.

This morning, standing at the front of my high school math class, I feel an even stronger connection to my students. And I feel in control. Numbers—they do not lie to you; they do not let you down. I explain the first problem, my eyes scanning the classroom, counting students. Someone is missing. When I'm presenting the second problem, Xavier stumbles in, limping slightly and with his left eye blackened.

I don't ask him for his late pass nor for his homework. I even let him read whatever it is he's awkwardly hidden behind his math textbook. A large oval bruise on his upper arm is already aging, turning from black to green. As I answer a student's question, my mind goes through a familiar set of choices: the police, youth protection, the *directrice* of the school... When the authorities were called in last time, it did not end well: denials by Xavier and threats of legal action by his politically connected family, followed by months of unexplained absences and hidden punishments.

I ask Xavier to remain after class is over. He approaches my desk, giving me a sullen look from under his long hair. There seems little point in asking him what happened, so instead, I ask him what he's reading. He hesitates, then shrugs and places it in my hand.

"What is it?" I ask.

"*C'est une bande-dessinée.* 'Comic book' in English."

"I am not anglophone," I say.

"Yeah, but you're not from here, are you?"

He says this like I might be from Mars or some other planet.

"Why do the people in the *bande-dessinée* have the heads of animals?" I ask. "Are they superheroes, these animal-headed people?"

"I'm not ten years old. I don't believe in superheroes."

"I would like to help you, Xavi."

"I don't need anyone's help. And I can't stay. There's a student union meeting. To vote on the strike."

Enthusiasm has replaced his precocious cynicism.

"*D'accord.* I will see you in class tomorrow."

He taps my raised fist with his own, smiling indulgently, like to a younger or more naive brother. I watch him try to hide his limp and immediately feel depressed.

The end of the day finds me in the teachers' lounge. Luc joins me, compositions from his students clutched in his big hands. I gaze up at my best friend and he quickly drops down beside me.

"*Qu'est-ce que tu as?*" he asks, reading me as always.

"Xavier came into class today all beaten up. I don't know what I should do."

"If you suspect something ..."

"It is beyond suspecting. I *know* what's happening and it's not just beatings."

"Are you sure of this?" he asks.

I simply look at him. He knows about my past. Not just the torture but the rapes as well. Luc was able to get this information out of me in a coherent way when even the tribunal could not.

"The only thing I'm not sure of is *who* is doing it," I finally say.

"Don't worry, Gabriel, we'll figure this out, I promise you. I have friends at youth protection. I even know a cousin of Xavier's mother. We'll find a way to help him."

I feel a little reassured. I move closer, so that my leg is touching his and I can lean against him. He lets me, even puts his arm around my shoulder. Some of the darkness leaks out of me.

If Arielle were here, she would be happy, seeing how I can still take comfort from other men. She was my lawyer at the refugee hearing and knows my past, accepts me as I am. She tried to prepare me for their questions, but I failed her. On such and such a date, they asked me, had I been tortured for my political crimes or for the crime of being queer? It seemed important to be precise about this, but I was confused. Maybe I was tortured for the former and raped for the latter. The fear of disappointing the officials, of making them angry, made my words flee. Perhaps that's why, in the middle of the hearing, I blanked out. When I came back, I was standing on a chair without any clothes on, turning around in circles as though to model my scars.

"I should go home," I say to Luc. "To cook supper. Arielle is counting on me."

"How is Arielle?"

"She is good. We had very hot sex last night. Do you want to hear about it?"

I feel happy thinking about this while leaning against Luc's shoulder. It was when Arielle and I made love for the first time, on the floor of her office, that I realized she had superpowers. I hadn't been sure before, even though she'd rescued me from the hearing, helping me to dress myself before bringing me to the hospital. Arielle might even have won my case, but instead, she found a way to spare me the pain of the hearing. She offered to marry me. Her colleagues teased that she didn't want to risk a blemish on her perfect record, but Arielle explained it all in logical, lawyerly terms. She'd just gone through another in a series of unreliable roommates and untrustworthy boyfriends. She wanted someone who shared her political values to also share, on a longterm basis, the household expenses and cooking. And one other thing. She wanted a child.

Luc tells me maybe another time, after a few beers.

"Will we go somewhere that has 'Maudite' beer?" I ask him. "I like the picture on the label, of the flying canoe, *la chasse galerie*."

"You're such a child sometimes. And speaking of children, I have that book for Raphaël. Of old Québecois tales, including a few *chasse galerie* stories." He hands me a large volume, the edges soft with use.

"It's beautiful," I say, running my fingers along the expensive binding.

"My parents gave me this collection. Keep it as long as you need it."

"*Merci beaucoup, mon cher ami,*" I say, kissing him on both cheeks and then once on the lips for good measure. He accepts my shows of affection with his usual aplomb.

That night, I tell Raphaël my own version of a *chasse galerie* story.

"Once upon a time, some men were chopping down trees deep in the winter forest. They were sad because they missed their children and partners."

"Where were the children and partners, Papa?"

"In another forest... planting trees to replace those that had been cut down. So one day, the men boarded a magic canoe to visit their loved ones."

"Were they superheroes?"

"*Claro que si.* They were very good friends who could... they could mix their powers together into one big superpower. That's how they made the canoe fly. But there was a super villain too, and he... he sprinkled forgetting dust into their eyes so that they could not remember who they were, and their canoe started falling down to the earth."

"Oh no! What happened?"

"Flying boy came to the rescue. He brought the boat down safely and used a magical washcloth to wipe the forgetting dust out of the men's eyes."

"Was Flying boy wearing his red cape?"

"Yes. And now it's time for superheroes to go to sleep."

"Papa? Why did the super villain make the men forget things? Why is he bad?"

"I don't know. Maybe a bad thing happened to him, something he needed to forget. Good night, Flying boy."

"Good night, Papa."

I tuck him into bed, trying to ignore a growing darkness. I make myself think of the night Rapha was born. The moment I held him, I knew he'd been gifted with strong powers and that it was my job to protect him until he was old enough to use them safely. This responsibility is what has kept me from ending my own worthless life.

Arielle is watching the nightly update on the student strike that reignited this fall. There's a late-breaking development about a student who's in critical condition after a plastic bullet struck her in the eye. I pull Arielle onto my lap and hide my face in her curls while counting to myself. Maybe Arielle will use her gifts tonight to make me forget things that strike and burn and tear into tender flesh. Maybe, at least, she can help me get a few hours of sleep.

On Facebook, I learn that this week has been declared *"une semaine de résistance"* for secondary school students. Our school votes to go on strike, but staff must report to work as usual. I stay in the teachers' lounge, not wanting to be alone, but I'm restless, so I go down the hall and stand at the entrance. At nine o'clock, the police arrive in full riot gear and declare the students' picket illegal. They open their trunks and pull out shiny yellow vests and canisters of malevolent substances. I walk back into the teachers' lounge.

"We should be out there," I say to the others.

A debate ensues but many teachers are missing, waiting in their classrooms.

"I'll get them," Luc volunteers. He turns to me. "Stay here until I get back."

I wait for a while, then go to the front entrance again and see the beginnings of trouble between a group of students and the riot cops. I wonder where Luc is and turn to see him right behind me.

"*Venez dehors! Nos étudiants se font embêter!*" he shouts to the others.

I run outside and Luc catches up to me, his hand closing around my upper arm. I pull him with me as I throw myself between the students and the riot police. We're shoved but keep to our feet and Luc is saying "*Calmez-vous, calmez-vous,*" making eye contact with each of the cops in front of us, patiently explaining that we are teachers, a French teacher and a Mathematics teacher, and that we must all remain calm to set a good example.

After a few tense moments, more teachers come outside. We join hands, forming a barrier between the students and the police. The students chant slogans like "Education is a right" and "À qui nos écoles? À nous nos écoles". Luc pulls *L'Étranger* from his back pocket and begins reciting from it. I spot Xavier. He's focused and intense, a courageous smile on his face. By the end of the morning, almost all of my colleagues have joined us and the police have retreated to their cars. I grip Luc's hand tighter and think about kissing every single teacher standing with us. With these heroes beside me, I feel invincible.

The next night I have a beer with Luc at a café on rue St. Denis. I finish five 'Maudites' and am feeling a nice buzz from that, with its higher alcohol content. I told Arielle I'd eat something with Luc. I can't lie to her so I steal a handful of his fries. He offers me his burger but I shake my head, too keyed up to eat much.

"Shouldn't we be going?" I ask. "The *manif* is scheduled to begin at 21 hours."

"It's not like the theatre, my friend. We don't have to be there when the curtain rises. You sure this is alright with Arielle? There's more risk of being arrested at night."

"I have promised to be careful."

At Parc Émilie-Gamelin, I'm in my element. It's hot for late September. A thick darkness envelops me. There's an aura of unpredictability that I appreciate because deep down, I'm an optimist who believes that whatever happens next has got to be better than the shit we have now. My lips move to the chants. An anarchist marching band playing circus music draws me in deeper, to where the park is filled with magic.

Luc introduces me to people he knows. After a while, I wander off as he gets into conversation with one of his ex-girlfriends. There's a group of men wearing dark clothing on the fringes of the manif.

They're rowdy and loud and exude a dangerous energy. I'm drawn to them. I also want to run from them. I find myself a couple of metres closer to the group, though I don't remember deciding to approach them. In fact, I remember deciding the opposite. My feet are taking more steps in their direction and I can't make myself stop. The men are carrying something in their hands. Their eyes flash yellow in the darkness. I'm terrified and mesmerized as I come closer still. One raises his arm with a look of gleeful malice. Someone grabs my shirt from behind.

"*Câlisse de tabarnak*," Luc shouts. "Can't I turn my back on you for a minute?" My collar is bunched up in his fist as he guides me, not gently, out of the park.

"Who are those guys?" I ask. "They looked like skinheads with hair."

"*Agents provocateurs* or just assholes. What difference does it make? You know to stay away from them."

"They have evil powers. I couldn't pull away."

"You've had too many beers. It's time to go home."

I leave with him, but I know I'll be back tomorrow night and all the nights after. I've found another activity where it feels right that I'm still alive. I count through the list in my head: Taking care of Raphaël, teaching my students, making love, being drunk or stoned, going to *manifs* with a certain type of energy. I'll just have to be careful, to resist the evil power. It'll be worth it if we succeed. It may even give me back some of the life force stolen from me when I was a teenager.

Arielle and I are watching the news. She's become a news junkie in the same way that I've become a junkie for demonstrations.

"Our government makes me ashamed to be *Québécoise*," Arielle says.

"That is not Québec. The real Québec is in the streets, marching and chanting and demonstrating. Come out with me more. You would feel better," I tell her.

She touches my cheek. "*You* reassuring *me*. It should be the other way around."

Of course the police violence and new repressive laws frighten me. But conditions in Québec, politically and socially, are still better than in the country where I was born. It's for this very reason that whenever things become worse here, I feel nauseous, like the world is spinning in the wrong direction.

"Let's go together to the flashmob nude *manif* tomorrow. It will be fun. I can put *fleur-de-lys* pasties on your nipples."

She smiles and I know I've convinced her.

The next day, Arielle calls me at school to say that they're concerned about Raphaël at the *garderie*. He's telling everyone that he's a superhero and trying to fly off tables and playground equipment. They've asked for a meeting.

"I can go, Arielle."

"They've asked that I come, specifically."

"That is sexism."

"No, it's more that…"

"What?"

"It's because of what you told Raphaël, last time this happened. That he needed to wait until he was older to use his superpowers. And to only use them when they're needed… and other things they've heard you say."

"Are you angry with me?"

"No, not angry but… We'll talk more later. Are you still going to the *manif*?"

"Yes."

"There's usually less police violence at the nude ones. You'll be careful?"

"Of course. I love you."

Without Arielle and Raphaël, the apartment feels a little sinister. It's better in Raphaël 's room where I can sense him in his toys and clothes and artwork. I hold on to one of his superhero figures and draw strength from that.

In our bedroom, I lay down and wrap my arms around Arielle's pillow and breathe in her familiar odour. It's not enough. On the shelf in the back of my closet, I find the box that I haven't opened since my uncle smuggled me out of my country. I take out the red cape, red feathered mask and calf-high red boots. The cape against my nose, I smell the streets of my childhood and adolescence.

My mother sewed this costume, but she did not bring me up to believe in superheroes. My parents were university professors. Both were politically active, proud of my work for the student newspaper and tolerant of my sexual explorations. Their openness and support encouraged me to finally tell what my uncle did to me.

No, my parents did not believe in superheroes. Nor did they believe in super villains. Just because you don't believe in something doesn't mean it can't kill you. They never should have gone to the police about what my uncle did. They thought they could protect and avenge me but he was too powerful. Their so-called accident deprived me of protection. Thoughts of vengeance are like cold ashes in my mouth.

I hold the costume in my hands, remembering when I wore it so proudly. It was after "los casserolazos", after the occupation of the campus library, and after the kiss-in, but the taste of my classmates' lips was still fresh in my memory. The superhero demonstration was the last one before I was taken. Like me, only parts of the costume survived, but maybe some traces of the powers that were stolen from me remain in the material. I shove it into a bag and head for my bike.

I'm marching down rue Ste-Catherine wearing my cape, my boots, my mask and nothing else. The breeze ruffles my pubic hair. My boots protect my feet and my mask protects my identity. It's almost like having the power of invisibility.

Everyone is friendly, many people talk to me. A few ask for my contact info, take my picture. I know I'm good looking but I take no pride in this. I did nothing to earn my looks, yet, it's something I've had to pay for, repeatedly. "Excuse me," I say to the person who's been chatting with me for the last kilometre. "I have to stop here." On the side street under a circus canopy stands a man wearing a red kerchief who has the dark eyes and quirked smile of my country of birth. He's holding a six-inch tall toy polar bear banging a miniature pot with a tiny, perfectly formed wooden spoon. The bear is wearing the flag of Québec as a cape.

"How much, *monsieur*?" I ask.

"Just take it, *hermano*."

"I couldn't."

"Yes. It is for your child. Take it."

I hold the bear, sensing in its erect posture and soft gaze a desire to protect. I look up to thank the man, wondering how he knows about Rapha, but he's gone.

At home, I give Rapha his gift. I let him turn it on so that he can hear the pot banging, a sweet, high pitched clang clang... clangclangclang. I tell him to keep it safe because of its magic, then kiss him goodnight.

That evening, on Facebook, I see the first photo of myself at the nude manif. In the next couple of days, more photos follow, including one where my back is to the camera as I look over my shoulder. I'm holding up the toy polar bear with its flag-of-Québec cape. My other fist is raised as well. This is the photo that goes viral.

Wednesday, I arrive early at school and, uncharacteristically, so does Luc. He comes into my classroom with a copy of a popular glossy magazine in his hand. He slaps it onto my desk.

"Please tell me this isn't you."

I look at the cover photo—a close-up shot of me at the *manif*, fist in air, my more private parts artfully photo-shopped. It's difficult to answer him, the power of his verbal request at odds with the truth.

"He's wearing a mask," I finally answer. "You can't tell, for sure, who he is."

"*Je n'en reviens pas*. You can't be that stupid."

I hang my head thinking, 'Yes I can.' He hears my thoughts.

"*Écoute*, you're going to be called into the *directrice*'s office this afternoon. Don't say anything. Let me handle it. *D'accord?*"

At the meeting, Arielle is there too. Luc must have called her. They sit on either side of me, protecting me as they answer concerns about propriety, judgment, reputation, regulations. My head is pounding from the force of the words in the room. I try to count how many hours of sleep I've had this week. If I strung those hours together, would it be equivalent to one full night's rest?

In the end, I'm told that I've gotten off lightly. I'm told this by the *directrice*, by Luc and again by Arielle on the way home. I get to keep my job, without even a warning in my record. But I cannot come to work for ten days. The first day is without pay and those following are sick days for me to rest and "find my equilibrium". I am not to give interviews.

Still, the news is full of information about me—that I am a teacher with a four-year old son, that I am a refugee which, strictly speaking, is not even true. But this is the excuse used for why my school is not identified, nor my name used. The real reason is that Arielle and Luc have created a shield of partial invisibility.

Nevertheless, there are photos of me—far away, obscured, fully clothed. And quotes in support of the movement and against police violence, not attributed directly to me but said to be "summaries of my position" as communicated to "friends". I learn that the fact that this message comes from a good-looking, naked teacher who is also a political refugee and father has earned me, and the movement, "a great deal of new popular support." Arielle tells me that this has earned me a lot of enemies too—principally, the government and the police—and insists that I lay low for a while.

I try to do as Arielle says. For the first forty-eight hours, I actually do not leave my bed. Arielle suggests I start seeing my therapist more frequently. Luc comes by with offers of bike rides, soccer games, a film. The problem is that I am not teaching, not with my students. When Raphaël is at the *garderie*, I feel useless. Finally, I tell Arielle that I must get out, if only to bike around the city.

The next day, I participate in three separate demonstrations and a teach-in organized by professors. Afterwards, I go to a public *assemblée générale*. The meeting is held in Parc Lafontaine where, just metres from us, a woman in black fishnet tights and stilettos is being taught to wield a whip by a huge bald man in leather. Every few minutes, I'm distracted by the sound of the whip cracking accompanied by a sharp burning pain on my back, but when I look around the assembly, no one else seems bothered. It occurs to me that I may be the only one who can perceive these two super villains. I leave and, biking very fast, attend seven different *"casserolazos"* before heading to the night *manif*. When I return home, Arielle asks me what I've been up to. I tell her everything, which of course I must do. She seems deeply disturbed and insists that we both stay home the next day.

It's a good day. We make love, nap, drink red wine. I feed a little off her life force—I cannot help myself—but I don't think it hurts her because she's so strong. In the evening, I put Raphaël to bed while she listens to the news. She's turned the volume low but I can tell there's been a report of some super villainy. I know this by the staccato rhythm of the words, the erratic, fractured images. As I enter the living room, Arielle turns off the television. I walk towards it as though to a cooling corpse.

"What happened?"

She hesitates. "Some arrests, police violence. There were… injuries, that's all."

I know that I'm to blame. I either caused it or… or maybe if I had been there, I could have lured the evil towards me.

"I'm going to the demonstration tomorrow," I tell Arielle.

"Gabriel …"

I cut her off, steel myself against her power.

"Please," I say, putting my fingers on her lips. "Please," I whisper again.

She sighs. "Then I'm going too."

On the way to the demonstration the next morning, we drop Rapha off at his friend's apartment on avenue Mont Royal. He's disappointed that he can't come, but we tell him to watch for us, that the march will pass right by his street.

After last night's events, the mood at the grand *manif* is somber. The numbers of police and the way they are armed seem more a provocation than a way of keeping the peace. Nevertheless, the demonstrators remain positive. I march between Arielle and Luc in a bubble of safety. Something in the mood still doesn't feel right, though. I'm glad that Rapha is safe at his friend's home.

It's after crossing St. Laurent that I realize the super villains are trying to take control of the demonstration. I can see them, just off to my right, but whenever I turn my head, they're gone. Arielle asks me what's wrong, so I mention my nervousness for the students. Luc thinks I mean *our* students and says that he saw Xavier and other kids from our school marching with a youth contingent behind us. He offers to try to find them for me and to talk to Xavier if possible.

Now there is only Arielle beside me. This is the moment when I must leave. I kiss her hard on the lips and make a run for it. I find them easily, instinctively, the evil calling out to me. I can taste the violence in the air as it draws me closer. Suddenly, I see Xavier in front of me and feel a sense of mounting panic.

Everything happens at once. An arm is raised. People are running. A canister bursts in the air. Riot police appear from nowhere, weapons already in hand. Arielle calls me from a distance, Luc's head and shoulders appear above the crowd far behind me. The mass of humanity is rumbling and reforming. Xavier's eyes meet my own.

"Run!" I yell to him and his friends, and they do.

The next instant, the first *matraque* cuts across my hip, taking my legs out from under me. My head hits the pavement. Everything goes dark. I remember.

We were all standing under the night sky, a mass of students dancing in our superhero costumes. The evening was hot and full of motion, my arms tight around the shoulders of my two best friends. We sang and danced while we waited for the government to finally see that we were their children and that the things we fought for were good and right and pure.

I was almost too happy, too excited. Almost, I was a little bored. My two friends agreed to leave with me and we found our way to my old home. Someone had placed a new lock on the door I used to enter. I was seeking my parents' ghosts, hoping they were watching over us, yet I did not heed this obvious warning from the dead. I smashed the window, my parents' murder a shard in my heart.

We were inside, kissing. I went from one set of lips to the other, my hand under the girl's superhero skirt, the other rubbing the boy through his superhero tights. It was all very innocent—cuddles and caresses, seeking warmth in the ruins of my childhood home. I thought about returning to the demonstration, guilty about convincing my friends to follow me to this dark and sad place. This was the power that I had—to make people love me, to make them see my love for them, to make them follow me, heedlessly.

And still, It might have been alright, if I hadn't taken off my costume.

My eyes snap open. The cop's face is snarling above me. "It's you, the magazine star. Let them take your picture now," he says, punctuating his words with a blow across the chest. I taste blood in the back of my throat.

They arrived with their guns, pulling me from my friends. The beating began at once, the force of the blows seeming to flow from an exterior power. I fought back at first, scanning the street outside for help. When my uncle stepped forward from the darkness with a look of anticipation about to be satisfied, I stopped fighting.

"Run!" I yelled to my friends. And they did.

I don't want to fight back this time. But my body doesn't listen to me. It's trying to stand. The next blow takes me and I'm on the ground again, the pain exploding behind my eyes and trying to spread itself more evenly throughout my body. I look up, hoping they'll finish me off quickly. It's then that I see Rapha leaning over his friend's balcony, the little bear clanging away in alarm, my son's mouth a big "O".

Pain. The stench of death and decay. In the prison, my only comfort was that my friends were not also taken. I balanced this against my agony. Snatches of sleep are brief, dreams of warm lips and smooth limbs. I began to imagine that I could see my friends flying over the prison in their costumes, planning to save me. I waited for rescue as minutes/hours/days became lifetimes endured. My uncle always came after the pain, speaking to me of loyalty to government and family and God, his hands on my body, gentle as a poisonous eel. Bled and pumped dry, I could no longer hear my own cries. They'd stolen my life force and I was fading. I finally realized that my friends' superhero powers must have been stolen as well. That this is why they never came for me.

Raphaël has climbed over the balcony railing. With horror, I realize that he's seen me. I sense Arielle's presence coming nearer, Luc's as well. My death is coming too, but not soon enough. I will still be alive to see my child jump from the balcony.

"Rapha!" I cry as he becomes airborne, his cape flying out behind him. The police baton is raised again. I close my eyes and wait for it.

I'm flying through the air, holding on to Raphaël. We're moving very fast above the streets of Montréal. Am I dead yet? I don't want Rapha to be in a place of the dead. "No," I moan and realize that, after all these years, I can hear my cries of pain again.

"Shh," a familiar voice says. "*Ça va aller.* I've got you."

Luc's face is above mine, his arms carrying me swiftly through the streets, the crowd opening before him. If I could, I'd ask him to care for Raphaël in my place. My hand rests against Luc's chest, his shirt wet and sticky with my blood. I try to touch his lips with my fingers so he can read my mind, but my fingers reach only his chin, slipping down again on its rough wetness. My hand drops to my own mouth. I taste salt, feel Luc's chest heave with his sobs, with the strain of carrying me and running. I press my hand against his heart and he runs faster.

In the ambulance, Arielle holds my hand. Her voice cradles me. "*Lâche pas*, Gabriel. *Lâche pas*." Hope hurts more than giving up, though, and I don't think I can take any more pain. Then she puts my hand on her cheek and I feel her tears. I absorb the salt through the tips of my fingers and hold on a little longer.

Awareness slips in between longer periods of confusion. I see the friends from my student days beckoning me to dance with them. I see them pass the missing pieces of my costume to Arielle and Luc who hold fast with their powers of reason and strength, of goodness and loyalty. Above them all is my precious Rapha, flying and free. I remember now how he jumped from the balcony, landing squarely on the policeman's back, how he passed his red felt square across the cop's eyes, and how the man backed away from me in shock, as though only now seeing what he had done.

I wake and wake again. Luc or Arielle are always beside me holding tightly to my hand. When I ask for Rapha, I am told not to worry, that he is fine. I sleep and heal.

On a day when my head is clear, I open my eyes to Arielle sitting beside my hospital bed with Rapha on her lap. He clutches a newspaper, on the front page, a photo of his exploit, his red cape flying out behind him. The headlines reads: Boy superhero leaps to the rescue. Negotiations resume, student leaders hopeful.

"What happened?" I ask.

"It's a long story," Arielle says. "What did you think you were doing?"

"My students were in danger. I saw Xavier, told him to run."

"Well he ran and found Luc, which probably saved your life."

"Papa," Raphaël whispers. "Maman made me promise not to fly anymore until I am grown up. I said *d'accord* but only if you come back to life."

"Well I have, so you must do as you have promised."

"I also promised not to tell any more newspaper people about how I can fly. And about the magic forgetting dust."

"Forgetting dust?" I ask.

"Yes. Like you told me. I used the red square to wipe it from the policeman's eyes. And I said the magic words."

"What words, Rapha?"

"Je me souviens."

Lessons of the Sun

Sequel to "Lessons of the Moon" in *Accessing the Future* (2015)

Joyce Chng

The sun gives and takes away
Tears that trickle like
Spring water.

The sun burns and sears
The skin that coats my
Body.

The sun, oh the sun.
My sun revolves around the moon-memory
Of my mother
Lost in space.

My sun is a star that
Still burns
Somewhere.

Under the sun, I work,
Dig dig dig –
History speaks in the dirt.

My sun shines on silver pieces,
Like solidified tears –
And I know.

I just know that she is there
Wo ai ni.

I miss you, ma ma.
We miss you a lot.

Perhaps there are flower chains
In heaven.

Sophie and Zoe at the End of the World

Rebecca Buchanan

Ma usually cried when she watched the news. Not this morning.

She turned off the TV a little after ten; the static always gave her a headache, but she watched anyway. She carefully set the remote on the end table, and moved the black-and-white cat off her lap. Pushing herself off the couch, she announced, "Well, I guess that's it, then."

I followed her down the hallway to the bedroom, lingering in the doorway as she disappeared into the bathroom. The tabby came running out at her intrusion and rubbed up against my leg. The creak of the medicine cabinet. She came back a moment later, fingers lightly curled around a green bottle. It had a red cap and bright purple tape sealing it shut. Garish.

Her hands shook a bit as she ripped open the tape. Not fear, I knew, but hypoglycemia. Not like anyone was manufacturing insulin anymore; why bother? Off came the cap and she tipped the two black pills into her palm. One, two, into her mouth, and it was done, just like that.

She kicked off her shoes and laid back against the pillows. She flicked at her skirts, arranging them in neat folds. "Keep the door closed so that cats don't get to me," she instructed. When I didn't answer she lifted her head from the pillow. "You hear me, Sophie?"

I nodded. Cleared my throat. "I'm just—I'm gonna go see Zoe. In a bit."

"Oh, that's right." Ma dropped her head back down onto the pillow. Her words were beginning to slur and slide. Her breathing grew shallow. "She's leaving t'day, in't she?" Ma swallowed, breath catching. "Mother'd terrible taste, but Zoe knew the good shtufff…"

One breath, two, still, gone.

I picked up the tabby, hugging him tight. He mewled in protest. "Sorry," I whispered, but didn't let him go. Casting one last glance at Ma's still form, I pulled the bedroom door closed. The tabby mewled again as I made my way back down the hallway to the living room.

The grandfather clock gonged. Already ten-thirty. I dumped the cat on the couch, where he curled up next to his buddy. Zoe would be leaving soon. I didn't have much time.

I found the heavy canvas backpack in the box of camping supplies in the garage. After the grocery stores started to run low on food and the neighbors raided our garden, we'd had to dig into the box for MREs. There were only a few packs of fiesta chicken and powdered soup left. I grabbed those, too, in case Zoe might need them. After she woke up.

In the living room, I paused before the wall of bookcases, the bag dangling at my side. Ma and Zoe and I had spent ten years trolling library sales and garage sales and used book stores, looking for the best stuff, the weird, wonderful stories—"literary salvage ops," Zoe called them. I studied the shelves now, hunting the best and weirdest and most wonderful of them all.

I started with the picture books, gently pulling out a stained copy of *The Epic of Alexandra* by Dorothy Dayton. I ran my fingers over the cover and down the spine, inhaling the scent of chalk dust and erasers. The first day of kindergarten, Zoe had spotted me hiding the book under my desk while Mr. Applethwaite droned on about addition and subtraction. She didn't tell on me—but she did sit next to me on the bus ride home and insist that I share. I hugged the book, then set it gently in the bag. Peter Brown's *The Curious Garden*, *Imogene's Antlers* by Small, Jay Williams' *The Practical Princess*, and Munsch's *The Paperbag Princess* followed.

I raided our science fiction collection next. My hand hovered, finally settling on the battered copy of Le Guin's *The Dispossessed*. Varley's *Wizard* and Piercy's *He, She and It* and Russ's *The Female Man* followed, tumbling into the bag. I shook the canvas sack to get them to lay flat. I impulsively added an Octavia Butler collection, Delaney's *Trouble on Triton* and the Vonnegut omnibus, and moved on to the poetry shelves.

I bypassed all the classics—Homer, Sappho, Dante, Rumi—they would already have been packed away and shipped out to the facility by the government; the **safe** stuff. No. I needed the poems no one else would dare to take along, the weird renegade rebel verses. The **thinking** poetry. The Dickinson omnibus; yes. It thunked as it landed in the bag. The tabby meowed in irritation. *Diving Into the Wreck*; yes, Rich was another must. Thunk. I hesitated over *Ariel*, ultimately bypassing it in favor of Valente's *A Guide to Folktales in Fragile Dialects;* Zoe found that for me at a library sale for my twelfth birthday. I sniffed the cover, inhaling deeply. Thunk. Parallel french-english editions of Wittig's *Les Guérillères* and Baudelaire's *Les Fleurs du mal*. The illustrated *Walk Now In Beauty* by Canan and the beat up hardcover edition of Kennedy's *The Witch's Dictionary*.

The bag was getting heavy.

I moved on to the philosophy books. Again, I skipped the classics, the safe status quo stuff. Stirner's *The Ego and Its Own* went in the bag. Tucker's *Liberty*. A scarred hardcover edition of the *Collected Works of*

Voltairine de Cleyre. A near-pristine edition of Rose Wilder Lane's *The Discovery of Freedom*, which Zoe and I had found at a garage sale just a few months ago... People seemed to want to get rid of stuff, now. We'd traded a small bag of fresh peppers straight from the backyard for the book.

The clock gonged again. Eleven. Hurry.

I made a quick pass through the remaining book cases. *Grimm's Grimmest*; none of that bowdlerized crap for me and Ma and Zoe. Pullman's *His Dark Materials* omnibus, Hopkinson's *Brown Girl in the Ring*, Silko's *Ceremony*, Abbey's *The Monkey Wrench Gang*, and—I couldn't resist—*Pilgrim at Tinker Creek* by Dillard.

I tied the bag closed and snapped the flap shut. I left the door to the garage open, whistling for the cats. They ignored me until they heard the rattle of their food bucket. They wove between my legs while I mixed in a few teaspoons of rat poison. I set their bowls down, scratched their ears good-bye, and left them purring.

Staggering under the weight of the bag, I hefted it onto my back, pulling the straps tight across my chest. Inside, I heard the clock strike eleven-thirty. I grabbed my bike, tipping it upright, and flicked the garage door button. I glanced up. Streaks of odd-colored lightning flickered high in the atmosphere.

I clambered onto the bike, not bothering to close the garage door behind me. Wobbling, I found my balance. Pedaling hard, I tore down the street. Passed the abandoned cars and houses with yellow tape across the front doors. I could smell smoke. A sharp right. A dog raced up, barking madly and snapping. I wobbled again. I kicked at the dog and pedaled harder. Shallow left and down a steep hill. The dog fell behind, still barking. Applying the squealing brakes, I wove in and out and around cars and trash cans and trucks and debris. The street finally cleared out at the bottom of the hill. A functional car roared passed me, horn blaring.

I shot an obscene gesture at the driver and headed left. Zoe's house sat on the right side, five doors down.

A parade of vehicles had just pulled up in front. A big fancy bus, the windows darkened. Four jeeps filled with men in fatigues, rifles sticking over their shoulders, pistols at their hips, helmets on their heads. They clambered out of the jeeps, circling the bus, eyes wary. In the front lawn, near the curb: Zoe. Her mom. Her dad. Her brother Kyle, hugging a black suitcase covered in football team stickers. As I drew closer, I saw the bright white, laminated social security cards carefully pinned to each of their jackets. Curtains flickered in the windows of some of the neighboring houses.

The brakes squeaked as I slowed, turned into a driveway and onto the sidewalk. Zoe's head whipped around, her long black pig tails flying. She was wearing the navy blue ribbons I bought her for her tenth birthday; they were stained and tattered from constant wear.

"Sophie!" She dropped her bag and dashed over, passed the glaring soldiers.

Her mother reached for her, hissing. "Zoe! Zoe, get back here!" Her father picked up her bag and stepped towards the bus, ignoring us.

I dropped the bike and she threw her arms around me. She smelled of blueberries and cream. I inhaled deeply, holding the scent in my lungs. Her breasts pushed against mine, and I tightened my arms around her back, feeling the sweep of her shoulder blades. Her laminated social security card poked my collar bone.

"I was so afraid you wouldn't make it," she whispered against my neck. "I was afraid they would take us away and I wouldn't get to say good-bye."

"I'm here, I'm here." My voice caught and I had to swallow. "I'm here. I brought—um—" I pulled away a bit and she dropped her arms, taking my hands "—I brought the books. I grabbed what I could..." My voice trailed off as she smiled at me, dimples appearing on either side of her mouth. Her eyes crinkled. She raised her right hand, pinky out and slightly bent. I matched her gesture, wrapping my finger around hers and for one moment, one sweet moment, it was just us.

"Zoe!" her mother hissed again, stamping her foot. "We are leaving! Get over here!"

The dimples disappeared and Zoe's mouth twisted into a grimace. Over her shoulder, I saw her father climb into the bus, dragging her little brother by the hand. Kyle got off a half-wave before he disappeared inside.

I unclipped the straps and pulled the canvas bag off my back. It thumped to the ground between us. "I brought what I could," I repeated, babbling. "Ma wasn't—Ma couldn't help me pick." Zoe's eyes widened, then darkened with grief. Her fingers tangled through mine, around the straps. "So, I grabbed the best. I hope you like them."

"Dickinson? Grimm?"

I nodded, trying to smile. "Dayton, too."

She grinned, crying. "I traded for some Wonder Woman comics and snuck them into the bottom of Kyle's bag."

I could feel my nose running. "Oh, geez, your Mom'll hate that."

We giggled.

"Zoe!" Her mother was yelling now, impatient and embarrassed.

One of the soldiers came over. "Miss, we really do need to leave. The train'll go with or without you."

Zoe didn't answer, just nodded. I wiggled my hands free as she grabbed the straps and slung the backpack over one shoulder. She almost fell over. She couldn't let go so I cupped her face in both hands and kissed her. Our first and last kiss. She tasted like tart blueberries.

"Zoe!" her mother shrieked.

I slowly released her mouth, dropped my hands and stepped back. My heels banged into the bike. She was crying. I took another half step back, crossing my arms over my chest.

The soldier touched her shoulder, slowly turning her around. With his free hand, he tipped his hat at me. One step, then another, then another, away from me, the soldier following along beside her, his hand on her shoulder. Eyes red and furious, her mother shot me one more poisonous glare and then stormed onto the bus. Zoe stalled at the bottom of the steps and the soldier gave her a bit of a push. One step up, two, gone.

The soldiers clambered back into their jeeps, the doors hissed shut, and the bus rumbled to life. A plume of grayish exhaust and the parade took off down the street. I watched until it reached the intersection far, far down the road and turned right, vanishing.

An hour or so to the train station, to one of the few functional platforms. Five hours to a black spot on the map in the middle of the mountains. A few more hours to check in, carefully lock away their possessions, and then sleep. A long sleep, long enough for the storms to pass and the sun to calm and the planet to heal.

I bent and set the bike upright. She would dream of me, as I would dream of her in those last moments as I lay down next to Ma and swallowed those two black pills.

Accessing the Future

Kathryn Allan

Dear friend,

I discovered the strangest, most beautiful old book the other day at my grandparents' house. It is called *Accessing the Future* and there is a woman floating in space on its cover. At first I thought it was a book about the theory of time travel (it was published before Butler made her time-space breakthroughs) but it turns out that it's a collection of stories of people imagining what the future will be like. And all of the characters in the stories are disabled! There are even illustrations of people who are missing limbs and talking with retro-looking technology (I mean, really, there are quaint pictures of hand-held devices!). The twenty-first century was so weird.

I flipped through the book, just reading bits and pieces, and, wow, people used to worry about access. Such a funny sounding word. I kept saying it out loud to myself. Axe-sess. Ack-sssss. Like having a snake surprise you by crawling up your pantleg. I don't think that it meant the same thing to people then as it does now. I mean, access is just access to… whatever we want now. But apparently back then lots of people struggled with getting to places because there were all of these different barriers in their way. So impractical! Who designs a world where only some people can go? There wasn't the same sort of support available, I guess. And it kinda seems like a lot of people were just rude and clueless! They didn't even know how diverse human neurology is, and there was all of this anxiety about what was "normal" or not.

Anyways, the book is fascinating for its early understanding of disability. I'm sending it to you—let me know what you think.

Khartyn*

Dear Khartyn,

What a lovely, decadent, so appropriately retro surprise to receive a drone package containing the original paper copy of your grandmother's old book! I started out flicking through the pages, as you did, and couldn't resist reading a few of the stories all the way through. Wow yes, it is a real history lesson, isn't it? It's like they were pretending to write about the future, but they were really just getting angry about their present. It's kind of beautiful.

I liked the catsnake and the genetically engineered dragon: they're kind of like the sort of thing the Vitales would have crafted—before it was legal and they got bored of it. (Did they do that sort of thing in those days, or were they just writing magic, do you think?) And did you notice how the eight illustrations are all really telling the same story, if you ignore the pages in between and shuffle them into a different order! A secret graphic novel?

We need to be a bit careful not to overcongratulate ourselves when we look back at the primitive customs and prejudices our grandparents' culture still practiced, and assume that everything's fine now, that we've got everything right and there's nothing left to fight for. Think again about what you said about "access" being to "anything we want." Who has access to everything? Who doesn't? Why not? Who decides? Seeing how much we've achieved since these stories were written fills us with hope that things can get better, but it shouldn't mean we stop trying to become *even* better!</lecture>

I'm sending you the book back, not because I don't think you've made a copy (I have!) but because there's something about reading it from 100 year-old paper that I know you get a kick out of. And I want to hear more of your thoughts about the contents.

Your friend,

D.J. L!bri

Dear D.J.,

Thanks for sending *Accessing the Future* back so quickly (I didn't make a copy because I was too excited to show you—thank the speed of drones!). You're right, I'm taking the privileges that I have today for granted. My mothers always tell me that I'm lucky to be space-born and that things were and still are different for people who live on Earth. I know that other people who have my type of chronic pain don't always have the same medical care that I do (and can you imagine that it was once common to have *to pay* for medicine?).

I've now had time to read all of the stories and I totally overlooked the angry-at-the-present part. I guess I don't like to think of so many people struggling when there really was no good reason for it. I found the stories about working for revolution, about using one's own body as a weapon for change, inspiring. And there's a lot of humour in the stories too—if only they knew then how popular space pirates would become (speaking of which, have you seen the latest ep of *Janeway and the Seven Stars* yet? So good!).

I wish there was a way that we could go that far back in time and tell everyone that things will get better. That they don't have to worry about losing what makes us human to technology (I think it just makes us more interesting and more capable to do what we want). I think I've come to really love this strange old book. I'm used to seeing people like me and families like mine everywhere but it wasn't always that way. *Accessing the Future* must have been really important to the people who created and read it. I'm thrilled that you are into figuring out this book too. If you have any more insights into what's going on in it, tell me!

All good things,
Khartyn

Dear Khartyn,

You read the whole book! That's exciting... I've been basing my grandiloquent and sweeping statements on the few stories I mined and the pictures I read. I'm going to try to be more methodical to keep up with you.

You're right, there is a lot of humor in here—the third page of the graphic story where the children steal the alien pet made me laugh out loud!—and it's not just an angry book, that would be boring, I just meant that it was a book about then (their *now*) not an attempt to write a book about now (their *one day*), just as the "historical" casts that cool kids today all love so much are more about now than they are about then. Also, some of the stories would have made me angry if I had to live through them.

And I love the beauty that anger provokes, it's a sort of poetry, a violence of the mind that explodes expectations and lazy assumptions, that makes a mockery of bland realism, a savagery of banal reality and a travesty of benign credence. Rage allows the best writers to turn despair into hope, fantasy into resistance, tragedy into community, controversy into refusal to go quietly. This book is richer than I realized. Shall we talk more about the individual stories one at a time? (I'm not saying that because I'm too lazy to read them all at once, but because I think they *deserve* that kind of slow attention.)

What do you say? You pick the first story, and we'll compare notes in the next letter. Thanks so much for sharing this little archaeological treasure with me!

Peace,
L!bri

Art Attack!

Mark Harding

Fraxie says: There will be casualties

It is a typical—if crowded—Clydeside pub in the Glasgow docks. Dark tables spotted with the bright yellow of freshly squeezed orange juices and—for the more reckless—a scattering of Cappuccinos. And, of course, there is the silence.

There are a few ancient plasma screens on the walls, specially turned on for the launch. But of course, no one is watching.

Everyone is goggling their v-pods, everyone silent and still, except for lips that sporadically synch to the words in their heads, or twitch, to show the lip owner's thrall. Only the occasional appearance of a voiced hologram sprite trying to wean punters to a new pod channel disturbs the librarian hush. In this silence, a silence that smothers most of the world, Art Official Intelligences vast and cool and unsympathetic, regard their audience with algorithms and art analytics, and surely and instantly draw their plans. With a perfection that is both certain and exquisite, they dance human emotions like angels on a pin, dominating the minds of their masses for the mass of their time. Resistance is futile. Victory is total. The human 'creatives' have all gone to the wall, outperformed, outclassed, and decidedly undercut; there's not even an underground resistance. Except...

Two people break the silence, giggling at private jokes. Frank and Maxie, two secret artists with a mission, partners in crime, management accountants on the lash, happen to have crossed town to be in this bar on this night.

Frank is wearing kid-leather bucket-top boots, pink Bermuda shorts, a Paolazzi print silk shirt, green silk cravat, electrically heated socks and his new cashmere Edwardian frock coat, which he keeps on, so that he can stroke it whenever he feels the need.

Maxie has flung her parka on the floor, revealing a dress made of bubble-wrap, coming apart in several fetching places; the outfit is completed by black vinyl stockings, scarlet pixie boots and a set of flashing blue LEDs decoratively arranged in her hair.

To the casual observer, if there had been one, their appearance would not stand out from the crowd—except perhaps, for their face furniture. Frank has a pink 'sex-slave' mask perched on his faux-scarred forehead, while Maxie is sporting two pirate eye-patches at the ready on her brow.

Oh, and where are they hiding their v-pods? And are those beer bottles in their hands!

200 euros for a bottle of beer? Frank had exclaimed. *Not bad for this part of Glasgow.*

The couple have bagged the window with the best view. The *Test Tube and Baby* public house is one of the oldest buildings in The Sheds—the maze of streets and service blocks that have consumed the car parks around what used to be the Science and Exhibition Centres. The pub is squeezed like a bunion to the foot of the Glasgow Tower, which after 13 attempts and at 200 times the original build cost, can now safely swivel in the wind with the best of them. By pulling their heads back, Frank and Maxie can stare straight to the top of the Tower. Or they can look across the river to the equally high, dazzlingly lit sheds, which are the home of the Clyde Zeppelin Yards.

It's almost time. Maxie signals to Frank and goes off to flush something important down the loo. But at the crucial moment Frank is distracted by the alert chimes from his old-fashioned c-pod. Excitedly he scans his favourite blogs for their comments on the latest wave of Fraxie spam and graffiti. He's hardly registered that she's gone. The idiot! One second is all they need. Vulnerable without his wingwoman, Frank lets his unprotected eyes flicker about him. The art networks pulse in anticipation, pre-emptive diagnostics run wild: sensors self-tune and routers clear traffic to make way for the up-coming spikes.

One of the two mysterious targets whose disposable income far exceeds traceable expenditure, one of the last of the recalcitrant: Frank has left himself defenceless. The Art Intelligences fall, like raptors to their prey.

| Fraxie says: Perfection is the enemy |

Perfume first: a sensory sortie underneath Frank's conscious guard. Then vision. The holo-girl that appears in front of Frank is—no other word for it—perfect. There's no denying the sexual element, but we're not talking anything crass here. We're talking the equivalent of man-years of patient, steady, psycho-shopping-emoto-predictive techniques at their most sophisticated, targeted on a man of closely tracked cultural attainment and rated in the highest possible percentiles of both sensitivity and taste. And the girl's a babe...

The sprite smiles bashfully, wriggles her fingers charmingly and launches into a song of such sweet sadness it could make stones weep and traffic cops stay their tickets. Accompanied by music that Beethoven would have given his ear trumpet for, she steps forward with a grace that would have made Pavlova burst into tears, and gestures with a gesture that holds the whole sweet story of human love; to open the gate to Adam's lost garden. Golden light bathes across the oblivious inhabitants of the bar. Behind the sprite, Frank glimpses a faery glade of more enchantment than Keats had ever known, a greater Kubla Khan than any drug trip, a mystic realm: Rapture.

> **Subscribe? Green Yes or Red No.**

Only human, Frank lifts his right arm towards that oh-so-luscious glowing green icon.

"Tosser!" Maxie shouts. Running across the room, she pulls Frank's pink sleeping mask over his eyes and forces his hands over his ears. Pushing Frank behind her, she stares out fiercely at the holo-siren.

The sprite angles her head daintily, arches her lovely neck, throws a dazzling smile that fills the room with joy and warmth, catches Maxie's eye and extends her elegant hand.

Maxie too, reaches out slowly, nearly fingertip to touch fingertip, then jerks to the burning red blinking **No.**

"Die! Bitch!"

Pushes the button. And the sprite is gone.

She lifts Frank's eye-mask.

"That's twice this evening," she says, feigning annoyance to emphasise her concern.

"Sorry. You know I'm distracted today."

"You said that yesterday." But she kisses his eyes nevertheless.

It is time. As scheduled by the networks, all the v-casts in the vicinity of the Yards cease at the same millisecond. Stretching their limbs as if released from sleep, momentarily freed from ceaseless and perfect art, the Corporate partygoers blink at their surroundings, deafened by the silence, then babble into life and conversation. They each turn to their partner, smile reassuringly and wonder how long they must wait before returning to paradise.

It is time. Corporate pride is riding high. Mayor Sheridan, transmitting globally to the 1,239 civic and company employees required to drag themselves away from their v-casts, steps onto the podium at the base of the Glasgow Tower and addresses the (small) multitude.

Aargh... pride... aargh... great achievement...

Frank grips the edges of his delicious cashmere coat and wraps them tightly round Maxie's soft and popping body.

Aargh... European stage... aargh... economic vibrancy...

Pop! Says the bubble-wrap.

Aargh... age of communications... aargh... protecting the environment... aargh... aerial network... aargh... no need for satellites...

Pop! Pop! Says the bubble-wrap.

Aargh... largest in the world, piloted by advanced robotics... aargh...

Maxie finds the zip on Frank's fly.

... I name this ship: *The Graf Murdoch.*

Crash! Says the champagne bottle symbolically. Hurrah, the crowds mutter tepidly.

Zzzzzip! Says the zip.

The curtains of the great Zeppelin shed are slowly pulled open.

Like a fish, her hand moves silently.

Almost literally a machine from a dream, or a Magritte come to life, the giant Zeppelin swims out of its unlit lair. Nose up, and rising, impossibly gleaming like polished granite in the arc lights, the dirigible lifts upwards. Engines throb softly as it sensitively pushes its tip to the docking point at the peak of the Glasgow Tower.

Senses confused, silenced by the surreal, the crowds gasp.

Green laser lights bathe the delicate transmitter nodes dotted along the airship's skin. Searchlights throw harsh shadows on the high-voltage cables veining their way around the rigid frame. Like sparkles of blue labradorite, the flickering flashes of a hundred cameras reflect from the crystalline structure of the neo-ceramic fabric.

And then—bang! and the skin seems to burst like a sigh and everyone cries O! and Frank says O! and strange sparks fly about the sky like glow-worms and they flicker and fly like glow-words and in the dark sky they spill to spell

| *Humans refuse redundancy* |

and O! gasps the crowd and a stream of golden flares gush out and O! O! says Frank and

| *The Luddites were right* |

the glow-words say and the crowd begin to realise that the ship is moving strangely and the swirling orange ex-military-now-artist mini-drones peel back the dirigible's skin, exposing the shyly rippling gas cells like pink Victorian bloomers and the laser lights flash golden on the steel stripped bare, and white and blue sparks flash along the cables and the glow-words rain and change to burn demon red

> *Fraxie says: Revenge is a dish best served grinning*

And the little spent rockets squirm no more, auto-destruct, and fade like the dew, so soft, so Frankly O! and at last and now a a Ah!

In slow, flaccid majesty, crook-backed and shrinking, dribbling streams of ballast water, the deflating airship flops across the harsh angles of the hotel.

Zzzzzip! Says the zip.

> *Politics + Sex = Art*

Fraxie will say, or at least is planning to.

Vid-clips of the crash are uploaded by the few. The news of the amateur footage spreads to the many. The word is out. The world is up. Message to message, mail to mail chain across the hemispheres, fast as light. Official channels forgotten, humanity in millions hit the remaining free-server networks: posting, downloading, viewing, commenting, rating. Humanity leaving v-pods abandoned, sprites interrupted, shows unseen, dramas deserted, music unheard. And Oh No! Adverts unattended.

Like the Zeppelin, the pod viewing figures have dropped.

And a hundred art executives, at breakfast, at lunch, at supper, at home, in meetings, in cars, in beds, on wives, get their disaster alerts. The servers stayed up while the stock price has crashed.

And a hundred execs boot up a hundred pods and survey in dismay the wreckage. And wonder who the casualties are going to be.

And a hundred execs poll a hundred AIs and demand a recovery and demand an explanation. And try to pull some strings. And threaten to pull some plugs.

Of course, machines don't know fear. Of course, machines don't have pride. Artificial Intelligences make emotions they don't feel them; of course.

Maxie skips away from Frank and calls behind her: "I'm going up the Tower to get a photo of *The Murdoch* from above."

Fraxie says: There will be casualties

Status critical, audience share has to be regained. MIPs flop and flops cache and caches flip. Bandwidths blow, pages thrash, firewalls fall, processors pop. The servers stop serving. The resource managers de-source. Only one task matters, one total attempt at one instruction: Increase audience share; by any amount, by any means.

The AIs are fast. With each clock cycle they learn a little more. They learn that there's dollars in disasters. There's an audience in malevolence.

There's an incident: a mysterious virus penetrates the tower's computer. On a windless night, the tower's bearing engines needlessly kick in. And the tower starts swivelling, fast. And faster. Regardless of calculated performance envelopes, building regulations or EU restrictions, it spins too fast. And faster.

The plasma screens in the bar flicker; then pipe through the tower elevator's CCTV, speakers pick up the weird groaning of the tower gears. In black and white, Maxie is pressed against the glass, too breathless to scream, desperately looking for a last sight of Frank.

There's a loud crack from the base of the tower.

At last, they've got Frank's attention.

Slice of Life

Julie Novakova

Slice Of Life Pro is a new immersive game that enables you to experience one year of famous modern-age personalities' lifetime. Through meticulous research, we have reconstructed them most accurately. Due to our newest subjective time extension, you can live through a fantastic year in just two days of your time (Warning: Do not use for more than six hours consecutively. Mind your health and take breaks. We are not responsible for any damage caused by ignoring the instructions.).

Peer into the lives of Albert Einstein, Winston Churchill, Ella Fitzgerald, Kurt Cobain, Elizabeth Taylor, Truman Capote and many others throughout the late 19th and 20th century! Meet them as people just like us, see through their eyes and get a glimpse of their own lives, from the little details to big decisions.

Note: The app can be used as an educational aid in history, science or media lessons and is also recommended in empathy building sessions.

Tags: immersion, education, personalities, celebrities, empathy, history, biography

Reviews:

_____

Sean Parker

✪✪

The app is good but I was disappointed by the slice of Einstein's life it showed. Like, for real? He spent so much time having walks, socializing, reading outside of physics, rooting for political causes, playing music, blah, blah, blah. If this is really accurate, I'm the more disappointed—in him! If he gave less time to worthless pursuits and more time to his work, we could have been exploring the galaxy now!

_____

Timminator_3

✪

Took the Oscar Wilde slice, would fall asleep if wasn't immersed! Bored dead! Less sitting by pen and paper, boring!, more classy parties and lovers! Then I give 5*, yay!

_____

Gina F.

✪

Any chance of doing Paris Hilton next?

Keith Lark

✪✪

You made Steve Jobs totally uncharismatic, dudes!

Anna Novotná

✪✪✪

Miloš Forman se vám sice povedl, ale radši bych viděla jinou část jeho života než zrovna natáčení Valmonta. Přelet nad kukaččím hnízdem by byl lepší volba! Jinak ale chválím.

Francesca L.

✪

I tried the Frida Kahlo slice but I stopped after a month of it. I read a biography about her and she was like badass! You portrayed her like dull, guys, bad work!

Paul_Gibbs

✪✪✪

The Korolev piece was good. The von Braun slice made me very uncomfortable. Couldn't you have chosen the time when he was already an American?

Lynn Polanski

✪✪✪✪

I admire the beautiful graphics and the amount of research necessary for the reconstructions, also the effort to add more diverse personalities, even if it's just the first little step now. I chose the Martin Luther King, Albert Einstein and Emmeline Pankhurst slices. The description does not lie: you will see that famous personas were people just like us. Only that's where I think the problem is. After they die, famous people become ideas. Their legacy lives on and we make the mistake of identifying it with them. That's why we think we can understand them so much, even that we would have been best friends if we had lived in the same period. We forget to see them as complex people, recognize that they'd had other pursuits than what remained after them. I see how the developers thought the app would be good to promote empathy. But I'm afraid it serves this purpose only in those who wouldn't need it in the first place. I wish the devs good luck and hope I'm wrong.

Half Light House

James Bennett

Dark gables. Shadowed eaves. A man with a suitcase standing on the kerb.

Rain. Oceans of it. A leaden sheet to mask the world. Polished shoes in puddles. He pays the taxi fare. A smile that dies before it reaches the eyes and an ungracious 'thank you' in return. Welcome to England. Welcome home.

The sound of a leaf-throttled drain. The taxi swims away. His footsteps cross the street. A haiku on the air. A pause. Then mounting the steps to Half Light. One. Two. Three. They echo in the porch like a funeral drum. And so they should. So they should.

On the sanctuary of the porch, a reflection. It seems as though this is all there is. Three steps. Two Georgian pillars. A universe of falling water—and himself. The man once known as Lucas. The man *still* known as Lucas, though nobody really acknowledges it anymore. If he had friends, they would call him Luke. Surely. But he has no friends. People don't know him. Sometimes, he wonders if he is alive.

A door. A key. A dusty hall beyond.

And then, nostalgia.

Ten years to the day. When his tongue could stand the taste of gin. When his cock still got hard for magazines. Ten years to the day. When his patience could withstand small talk. When his eyes held a secret he didn't even know. A certain light only his mother and Falcon could see.

There are powerful dreams in there, his mother had told him when Lucas was nine.

Your eyes are funny. Falcon. In bed. The first time they made love. He was twenty-three. Ten years to the day.

I've never been like other men. Lucas knows this as he hangs up his coat and puts the suitcase down. Clunk. Drip. Sniff. *I never bloody wanted to be.*

And Falcon again. Always Falcon, with his colourless eyes and remarkable smile.

Thank God you're not, Luke. Thank God. If you're foolish enough to believe in Him.

Luke remembers lying naked in candlelight, perhaps on tarpaulin, perhaps not. Tracing a line on Falcon. Thigh to navel. To nipple, which he kisses. To navel again, then to cock. Falcon's exquisite cock. Always ready at a touch.

Luke shakes his head. The living room. Furniture draped in sheets. Piles of newspapers. Dust. All these sights create the memory. *Living* room. A strange expression. As if all the other rooms are dead. He catches the sob in his throat. Swallows it. Moves into the kitchen. He will not cry over sex. Love maybe, if he can recall it. Only love.

The kitchen. This is where he first met Falcon. Falcon the Artist. Falcon the Beautiful. Falcon the Dream Snatcher. Falcon the Whore. So many Falcons. A veritable flock. He may as well have been a Tarot deck. And that's what Falcon was doing, wasn't it? That day. The day Lucas set foot in Half Light House and left himself behind.

Do you play?
It's a Tarot deck.
Yes. Do you play?
I thought. Well. It isn't a game.
(Laughter. Sudden honey.)
You are new here. For sure.
Yes. My name is.
Luke. I know. I'm Falcon.
Falcon?
Yes. Do you play?
But.
(Laughter again. The kind of storm you want to get caught in.)
Luke. It's fate. Fate is a game, if anything is.
I.
Sit. I will read.
But.
Do you *play?*

Now. A scarred kitchen table. Then. Smooth mahogany.
Now. Luke sits alone and strokes the wood. Then. Luke sits down. There is no handshake. No other chat. Just his destiny being read by a total stranger.

The Tower. Beware a betrayal.
The Lovers. Possibly from a lover.
The Fool. Possibly from *yourself.*

Falcon's colourless eyes and archer's bow lips. Is that a pout? A smile? Hard to tell. Like everything was. Back then.

Now. Luke gets up. He can call himself Luke in Half Light. It's ok. The house knows him by that name. He walks into the garden. The ghost of a glass of wine in his hand. The sycamore tree. Falcon is standing a little too close. Maybe because he is taller. Maybe not. Luke moved into his room and paid the rent a week ago. Luke needs a job. Luke has come here to the town by the sea to search for—what? Yes, that was it. For (love) change. Luke needs change. He also needs Falcon to stop looking at him like that.

A sip of wine. A slant of the head.
Do you have a lover? Falcon makes it sound like an accusation.
No.
A pretty boy like you?
It's life.
Don't shrug.
What?
It *isn't* life.
Ok...
Luke.
Yes?
What do you want in a lover?
(Awkward laughter.)
I don't know.
Dream it up. Tell me.
Why?
So I know what to become.
(Awkward silence.)
Falcon. I'm not. I don't. I'm sorry.
I know. It's wrong. Against nature. God. The known laws of fucking everything.
You're bitter.
You're *lying.*
Please. Don't touch me there.
Kiss me.
I.
Kiss me.
But.

They kissed. A doorway opened. And later, flesh.

Now. Luke has climbed the stairs and stands in the bedroom door. The paint is flaking on the doorframe and the room is empty. Bare boards. No light bulb. Then. Luke stands uncertainly in the bedroom door. Red paint. Pink light. He has never been in Falcon's room before. He has never touched a man before. Now. He leans against the frame. A sigh. A tear. Back then there was a different kind of sigh. His cock was in Falcon's mouth.

Later, a cigarette. Shared. A cliché, but a good one. Luke is lying naked on the bed, tracing lines. He is trying to shake a feeling. The feeling won't leave him be. When he came, he thought the ground would open up and Hell would swallow him. It didn't.

I once heard. Luke hardly dares to say it.
Yes?
I once heard that.
Yes.
Someone told me.
Your father.
What?
Luke. Your father told you that to fuck like this is black magic.
How did you?
I can see it in your eyes.
But.
Your eyes are funny.
I.
Kiss me.

The memories are clear. Until he stepped into Half Light, he remembered nothing. Only a whisper. A rumour of something missing. Something stolen.

Now. Luke sits on the floor. He notices an old cigar box in one corner and crawls to get it. Then. He sees himself in a mirror of the pose. Naked. The last time they made love. Did he ever wear clothes in this room? No. Luke doesn't think so.

Falcon is speaking again. This is a month later in before-land. Luke is sore. He wonders if Falcon needs him. Is bored of him. Either of these.

I have given you truth. See?

That's your cock, Falc.
Yes. Truth.
I don't understand.
You don't need to. I want. I want something in exchange.
Here we go.
No.
You want my love. I don't know if I.
Hush.
(Those colourless eyes. An ocean you want to drown in.)
You don't want my love?
No Luke.
But.
I want the dreams.
What?
Your dreams.
I.
All of them.
Why?
To use. You go on now. If you can't give me that. You go on.
I don't understand.
No. They never do.

That last week. Falcon's scowl. Falcon's coldness. Until the last night ten years ago. In the living room where a part of Luke died. Fire in the grate. Jewels sparkling on Falcon's timeless face. Luke reached. Falcon withdrew.

I can't bear to do this. I have to touch you.
You are selfish.
No. I will. I will.
You will what?
Give you my dreams.
(Laughter. A lightning bolt you hope will strike you.)
Come here.
It's that simple?
Kiss me.
I.
Kiss me.

Then Falcon was gone. Life turned grey.
Joyless jobs. Speaking in crowds. Not being heard. Smiling at strangers. Frowns in return. Leaving Half Light. Leaving the town by

the sea. The stint in Amsterdam. The accident. The hospital. His best friend's death. Ten years! And all the time he was a shadow. Feeling nothing. Touching nothing. Tasting nothing. Fading. Fading. Faded.

Then the letter from Falcon. Three days ago.

I'm sorry. Go back to Half Light. Go back.

Now. Luke opens the cigar box. There is nothing inside but a note.

An absolution in twelve elegantly lettered words.

Your dreams are good. I give them back. Thanks for playing. Falcon.

A rush of light that isn't quite light.

A tingle in his chest and groin.

Then the sobbing comes for real. Luke wonders how much of himself he has spent in this room. In Half Light House. It's stopped raining. It's raining inside again. This time it's good. This time it's wonderful.

This time it's love.

Lifting the veil on the illustrators

Interviews by Cécile Matthey and Serge K. Keller

Illustrators usually work in the shadows, but they play a very important role in showcasing the stories. Theirs is by definition a solitary toil, striving to put their art in the service of the narrative. In the end, their work should catch your eye, make you dream or curious about the world you're about to discover.

An illustration is usually the result of a complex creative process. It involves not only the technical skills and experience of the artist, but also a sometimes strange and heterogeneous mixture of ideas, elements or events, that all contribute to making the artwork what it finally is. In short, behind an illustration there can be a whole world that you, the reader, may even not be aware of.

For once, we'd like to lift part of the veil to show you what lies « behind the scenes » of an illustration published alongside a story in *The Future Fire*. We've asked some of our artists to choose an artwork they made for the magazine, and to tell us a bit more about it.

You'll see that illustrators, who usually tell their stories through images, can also have very interesting things to say with words!

All the artists and links to their original images (in colour) can be found on the TFF site at futurefire.net/artists.

Eric Asaris

If I had to pick a favorite illustration that I've done for TFF, it would be for the story "I m d 1 in 10" by Victor Fernando R. Ocampo (*TFF* 2014.30). It's just such a superb story and I was intrigued by the character that Ocampo calls the Trip-Master Monkey. Was he a hallucination or an extradimensional entity? Either way, I saw the character as a bringer of wisdom in the form of an evolutionary ancestor.

When it came time to do the second illustration, I chose to do the old man pushing the ice cream cart. I reread the story and for reasons I still can't put my finger on, I decided to make the old man resemble a monkey.

There's nothing in the story to say that there is any kind of connection between the monkey and the old ice cream man, but that's just the way I saw him in my head.

Maybe it's because monkeys can be viewed as a reminder of our primitive ancestry, and the old man could be viewed as a relic or an obsolete person. The narrator sees him as a kind of dark warning. He will become like that old man—someone that society has passed by—if he doesn't join in with the herd mentality. Even when the narrator tries to conform to society he gets an even darker warning from the Trip-Master Monkey about what it means to be the One in Ten.

So maybe that's the connection. I don't know.

Anyway, Ocampo said the illustrations were "amazing if a bit disturbing." That's a rave review in my book!

Chris Cartwright

I loved doing all the illustrations I have done for TTF. The ones that stand out the most for me, however, are the ones I did for the story "Shadows in the Mirror" by Todd Thorne (*TFF* 2009.17). The main reason Djibril approached me to do this story was because of my experience with the subject matter. He knew I had spent time in virtual worlds, in fact he visited me there briefly one time! So this project was somewhat "personal" to me.

To create the art for this project, I thought it would be cool to actually go back into my "virtual reality" and get screen shots from there of my characters, and then take those images into Photoshop and create the art using those images. So, the three girls in the mirror were my actual characters. The lady looking into the mirror (Rachel), along with other elements was drawn in using a 3D graphic program and Photoshop.

There is more to the story of these characters, but that is an entirely different book!

Robin Kaplan

My "First last kiss" illustration for "Sophie and Zoe at the End of the World" by Rebecca Buchanan (*TFF* 2014.29) is one of my favorite pieces I've even drawn, for TFF or anyone else. I've written at length about it before in an interview/conversation with the author, but I'm not sure I managed to say much about my personal attachment to it.

I was just becoming a teenager in the nineties, and the apocalyptic rhetoric around the year 2000 was ubiquitous in the news and fiction I was surrounded with. It wasn't even a conscious thing I feared (I was far too logical)—it was just a tension at the back of my mind. At night when I couldn't sleep, I'd often think about what I'd want to be saved if all humanity vanished. It was always books. I wanted stories and poems and human thought to be preserved, because what is more human than that? My queer teenage yearnings for love were definitely mixed into this angst, too.

So when I read "Sophie and Zoe", I started crying and didn't really stop until I'd sketched the first pile of scribbles that became "First last kiss". The story was like looking into my darkest teenage feelings and I had not been prepared to go there.

Cécile Matthey

The illustration for "Bright Hunters" by Belinda Draper (*TFF* 2015.33) stands out for me because I managed to make it at once minimalist and expressive. Reading the story, I had immediately a clear picture of what I wanted to achieve: something dark, with a creature whose shape is only partially revealed by a ray of light coming through the darkness. From the text, the creature does not evoke a creepy sea monster, despite her tentacles, but a trapped animal, alone and afraid. I found a 19th century engraving showing fishermen catching a giant squid. The animal's big oval eyes gave it a naturally frightened expression, so I used this for my creature's face, to make her look fragile and touching, as she recoils from the menacing hunters' light.

The technique I used was a bit special. For the creature, I couldn't produce the effect I wanted through white paint or white chalk. So in the end I used a hard eraser to remove the black inked background in order to create the lighted areas that outline the creature.

The author liked this illustration so much she wrote to me to buy it. It was the biggest compliment!

Carmen Moran

If I had to choose one story, it would be "Bilaadi" by S. Ali (*TFF* 2012.22). This was not only my favourite set of illustrations, but also one of the most beautiful stories ever. I loved everything about it.

Around the time I was asked I'd just been working on improving my Photoshop skills, so this was my first real foray into completely Photoshop created illustration territory. I remember spending a lot of time looking at traditional (North-)African patterns and Nile fauna— the fish in the second picture was modelled after a Golden Nile Catfish, albeit in miniature, the real deal is a bit bigger...

I often get carried away with details in illustrations that I'm never sure anybody picks up on after the fact. Or maybe I just like to think I'm clever and mysterious over nothing, one or the other. Either way, for those who haven't spotted it, the tile corner designs behind the crocodile are made up of stylised frogs and fish, tadaa!

Anyways, well done on your ten years, TFF, here's to the next ten!

Drown or Die

Therese Arkenberg

"Marie Kilcannon is here to see you, ma'am," her secretary said from the door.

"Send her right in, Tom, thank you." Sharon replied without taking her eyes from the window. The rains that had come the past week had been heavy, almost as heavy as Earth's, she'd heard, and more of the trees in the arbor were rusting.

She would have to tell the gardener to plant more ornamental grasses. They didn't have the high iron content of the trees; like Earth's grasses, they had incorporated silica into their structure instead. The inundation of water into the atmosphere hadn't harmed them nearly so much.

"Sharon?"

Marie stood at the edge of the faux-fur carpet, her hydration mask hanging in one hand. Tom should have taken it with the rest of her suit, Sharon thought—but then she saw the chapped skin on Marie's slender arms.

"You came without a suit," she said. Not quite a question.

"It's not like I walked or anything. The way up your path isn't so long, not after a rain—anyway, I was in a hurry." A shy smile.

"I guess I was, too—I told Tom to bring you right in without giving you any time... here, let me take that." She lifted the mask from Marie's fingers and set it on the table.

"Your garden is beautiful this year."

"Thanks. Keeping it up has been hell. Terraforming's really started to affect it. I'm thinking of putting up a shield."

"Blocking the moisture out the way our home-shields lock the moisture in?" Marie's lips curled into a soft smile. *They* weren't chapped, but pink and faintly gleaming when her tongue ran over them. "That's clever, Sharon!"

"Thanks." Marie hadn't cared so much about the garden last year, her second summer on the planet, their first summer together; Sharon wondered what had changed. "If you bring a suit, maybe we can go walking in them next time."

"That would be wonderful." Marie's eyes had been on the windows, now they turned to her, and Sharon felt pinned beneath their dark, dark gaze.

"But, now ..." They met each other halfway for the kiss. Sharon's bedroom was upstairs, but she had a queen-size in the room beside the study, a holdover from when the distribution business was first starting up and she had worked until collapse some nights. Now it was useful for other things. She had left orders that when Marie Kilcannon visited alone, they were not to be disturbed.

Sharon was a native of Diana, had never been off the desert planet's surface in her life, and was perfectly accustomed to home-shields, iron trees, and hydration suits when the refugee ships arrived with their news of disaster. It was over for Earth, the climate had been shot to hell, and something like three billion Earth natives who had the resources to escape needed to be seeded out to the colonies. Colonies that, like Diana, didn't have the climate to support the population crush were to be terraformed until they did.

Speaking of shooting climates to hell...

Still, it was dry outside, despite the recent rains; dry because of the western wind that blew almost constantly, pitilessly from the vast desert plain. Lying sprawled on the polyester sheets, one hand tracing up and down Marie's naked back, she watched through the windows as silica-rough grasses bowed in the wind and a rust-eaten branch shivered brittlely.

Soon it would fall—even though the branches of Diana's iron trees were not supposed to, strong and solid as they were meant to be.

"Soon they'll be able to plant real trees out there," Marie murmured.

Sharon hid her wince. *Real trees*—like the iron trunks were just some creative sculpture. But Marie did care for Diana's somewhat-flora, in her own Earth-native way. She had been excited at the thought of a garden-shield saving them.

Sharon would have to set to work on that right away.

Marie sat up. "I'll have to head home soon or call Jacob."

"Call him. Tell him you're having dinner at my place."

"Okay ..."

"Or does he not like you seeing me?"

Marie gave her a quizzical look. "Of course, he doesn't know about *this* ..."

"But is he suspicious, or jealous just the same?"

"Of course not."

Sharon shrugged. Sometimes husbands could be like that. Wives too, no doubt, but she'd never had to worry about a jealous wife. "Then call him."

Dinner was simple, largely greenhouse-grown fare washed down by a vintage that had come from Earth—unimaginably pricy, it had been part of Sharon's estate long before the refugee ships arrived three years ago with the news that Earth would never grow grapes again.

Marie had seemed distant in the bedroom, and she wanted to find out why.

She sniffed delicately, almost cautiously, at the pale liquid Sharon poured in her glass. "Are we celebrating something?"

"You tell me." Sharon corked the bottle and sat back in her chair. "Or are we mourning?"

Marie's fingers traced the glass's rim. "I think I might be pregnant."

Sharon took a sip of wine, thinking. "That explains it. I thought you were acting oddly—well, hormones. Congratulations. So you're still sleeping with Jacob?"

The fingers stopped tracing, freezing like prey catching sight of a hunter. "I ..."

"God, Marie, I'm not judging you—he's your husband. I was just a little bit startled."

"You know I've wanted to have children."

"Sure, sure." She said it soothingly, trying to remove that look from Marie's eyes. Like a hunted animal. Or a guilty woman.

She'd wanted children for three years, ever since she and Jacob had arrived on Diana in the refugee wave—arrived alone. She had two sons and a daughter. One son had already been established on the Martian colony. One was sent to Prometheus, and the daughter went to Janus II. All sent separate places, the genetic heritage separated by light-decades as they were carried away on the refugee ships. The son on his way to Prometheus must still be in cyro-sleep.

"Well, it's what we're supposed to do here, isn't it?" Marie asked.

Sharon looked up from the tablecloth hem. "Sorry?"

"We're supposed to breed. Mix and match our genes. Create a viable population here."

"Sure."

"Jacob says he's thrilled. Of course. He knows it's what I want—and I wouldn't have slept with him otherwise, Sharon, promise—"

"I said it was no problem—"

"*But he keeps looking at me*—like I'm... unnatural, or something... like I'm trying to replace them!"

Sharon rose and went around the table. Put her arms around the shaking shoulders, let Marie press her face to her stomach.

"It's all right, sweetheart. Of course you aren't doing that. And he knows it—but this must be hard for him, I guess. They wer—they're his children, too." Encouraging empathy for her mistress's husband.

Well, she'd done stranger things.

"I know. I guess I know that. But thanks for telling me—thanks." She pulled back, wiping at tears with one hand and pressing the other to her flat stomach. "At least they're not going to send this one away."

Sharon sat back down. "I always thought that was bullshit, you know. Splitting up the families. So there's a little less genetic diversity on each ship, for each colony, but so what? *Family*, for God's sake. How desperate do you have to be to break that up?"

"Very," Marie said. And then they were quiet. They had an agreement not to speak of Earth.

They had to drown this planet. Drown it or die. They needed more oxygen, and for that they needed plants, Earth plants. And Earth's plants needed water.

And water was poisonous to Diana's ecosystem, but so what?

So what if your iron garden dies, Sharon? It's the future of the human race.

Bullshit.

It was Marie's fourth month. She still visited, though they didn't make love much anymore. In a way it was a relief to see their relationship was not only physical. There was also talking and walks in the gardens, though that last was also something they didn't do so frequently anymore.

"You really *should* get a shield for your plants soon, if you want to save them." Marie's eyes flashed behind her hydration mask. She was wearing a suit today, one she had put on after being reminded of the baby, though the climate was nearing the point where she could have gone without one and received only mild discomfort, provided there was no west wind. Today there wasn't.

Her child—a son, it was determined—would never know an atmosphere without water vapor.

"Yes, I should," Sharon said. If she didn't, Marie's son might never know a Diana with iron trees.

She had no excuse for procrastinating, except that every time she thought of placing calls and ordering a shield, she felt sick to her stomach. It was like getting a colon exam, or admitting defeat. Undignified, uncomfortable, and avoidable, no matter how necessary. Nothing forced her to get those shields.

Only the fact that if she didn't, the garden would die. And Marie would become very upset with her.

She looked now at the round curve of belly beneath the silver hydrosuit. Pregnancy *had* made Marie surprisingly sensitive—Sharon hadn't expected it. She thought all the rumored emotional changes were just legends, like PMS. Apparently not. This wouldn't be the first fight they'd had—about the trees, or anything, or nothing at all.

"You know what I *was* thinking of doing," she said, "I was thinking, in another month or two, of planting an Earth garden—cactuses and stuff, on the south side where they'll get a breeze off the new lake every once in a while. And I'll put up shields for when we get that west wind, at least until the west wets up. What do you think?"

"Cacti," Marie said.

"Sorry?"

"Not *cactuses*. It's cacti."

"Oh. Sorry."

Marie sat on the garden bench. It was iron, made to fit in with the trees, but Sharon had its surface treated with an anti-rusting agent after the first clouds formed. Sometimes she thought of applying the same agent to her arbor—it would kill the trees, by interfering with their chemical processes, but at least it would preserve the corpses. Carl, her new mechanic—new although she'd had him three years, a heavily in-debt refugee she had taken in out of pity—had suggested it. To Earth-natives, there wasn't much difference between a living tree of Diana, or a dead one.

"Jacob said he was going to plant a garden like that," Marie said. Sharon mentally kicked herself. "He says it'll be just like home. We're close, you know, to the new lake—our town council is thinking of naming it Terra. Lake Terra. I guess it'll be nice to see Earth plants again... although I'd like to see *real* trees. Oaks, maples. Jacob says they had the seeds in the holds of the ships when we came here."

"Maples are pretty, with their red leaves." Sharon faintly remembered some pictures, seen back in her school days.

"Sometimes they're green." Marie shifted. With her pregnancy, crossing her legs was becoming uncomfortable, but she wasn't in the habit of sitting any other way.

"Do you know what the population of Diana is?" she asked suddenly.

Sharon shrugged. "No. Something like two hundred seventy, three hundred million ..."

"Five hundred million. Because of the refugees from Earth. You would have gotten more, but the governments' coalition figured two hundred million was all the increase you could stand... It was three billion refugees, total. Earth's population was eight billion."

"I guess I never really heard."

"Five billion people were trapped—I guess they're still there—on a planet that's slowly becoming a toxic desert, because all the colonies together could support less than half of them. Nobody likes to talk about that. But do you know the absolute numbers of the human race? How many of us there are in the entire universe?"

"No ..."

"*Five billion*. That's it. The people on Earth don't count, that population's doomed anyway—so we're halved. Do you know, three hundred million was the kind of population an affluent country on Earth had in the *twenty-first century?* We've become practically an endangered species!"

Humans, endangered? Sharon looked away from Marie, over the rusting garden. The trees were an endangered species. One deliberately put in danger—for humans. "Well, you and Jake are doing your part to fix that up," she said.

"What?"

"Aren't you? Re-seeding? Creating a viable population? Spreading your DNA across the known universe?"

"Not by choice."

She pointed at Marie's abdomen. "Was that by choice?"

"*I didn't want to lose my children!*"

"Of course you didn't. I'm sorry. I didn't mean to imply otherwise. Please, sit down."

Marie sat down. "I'm sorry. I didn't meant to fly off the handle like that."

"It's okay." *Breathe, Sharon.* Deep breaths in and out. Diana's oxygen-faint air, lately enriched by some cacti and hardy algae, filtered through the hydrosuit. "You know, I guess I should start having kids myself sometime. The showtime ads—*Welcome to Diana, you're home, settle down and start a family*—are beginning to get to me."

"Don't be so bitter."

"What's there to be bitter about? It's the future of the human race."

"*Sharon*—" A gasp, funny sounds coming through the hydrosuit speaker—Marie's shoulders shuddered; she was crying.

"Sorry. Oh, Marie, I'm sorry, honey." She put an arm around the shaking shoulders, as close to an embrace as they could come in the hydrosuits. "I guess I *am* bitter."

"I just don't want this."

"Sorry?"

"I-just-don't-want-this." Marie sniffed and made as if to wipe her nose though the mask. "This planet, and the fact that we're killing it... and my kids... and Jacob's goddamn cactus garden, and now you... I want to go *home*," she said. "I want to go back."

"Oh, sweetheart." She rubbed Marie's back and let her head in its mask rest on her shoulder. "I ..." *I'm sorry? I love you? I'm sure it'll be all right?*

She said instead, so softly she was sure Marie couldn't hear, "I want to go home, too."

"Call for you, ma'am, Kilcannon residence."

"I'll take it in here, thanks, Tom."

"Sharon?"

She nearly fell from her chair—it wasn't the voice she'd expected. "Jacob? Hi. What is it?"

"Marie."

Oh, God. Hands kneading the edge of her desk, she said, "What's up? Anything wrong?"

"She's healthy... but Sharon, it's been hard on her. And... she doesn't know I'm saying this... she's always much happier after she's spent the day with you. And she and I, lately we just can't seem to get along... stress, I think."

"Sure," Sharon said. "And hormones."

"Well, I was going to ask... if it isn't too much trouble... maybe she can stay at your place a few days."

Sharon's mouth was open, and after a moment she realized the sound she thought was the halting hum of the humidifier came from her. "Sorry," she said. "I was just thinking ..."

"If it would inconvenience you, it's by no means necessary. We can make other plans." Jacob sounded testy—excellent, just excellent, she had offended him. Though she supposed with that sound she could hardly have done anything else.

"Sorry," she said. "I'd love to have Marie over. I'm just thinking of what I need to prepare—"

"We'll bring most of her things over. She'll be fine in a guest room, she'll cause you no trouble... er." Jacob cleared his throat, an embarrassed sound. "We're very grateful..."

"It's absolutely no problem." She smiled, because she'd heard such things carried in the voice. I should be happier, she thought. If nothing else, this proves he suspects nothing. "She can come over anytime. I'll have a room ready."

"Thank you." Jacob's voice was heavy with relief. "I know she loves being with you—I'm sure you'll do her good."

"Do you want to come outside?"

The shape at the window said, "No."

"Sunlight will be good for you."

"I can get sunlight here."

"Fresh air is good, too."

"Dry air, you mean."

"It's more humid now."

Marie turned to look at her with shadow-shrouded eyes in a face like a skull, drawn and pale. Her hair hung limply, uncombed, cleaned only when Sharon insisted. The last time she had done it herself, bathing Marie like a baby. All her body was like her face, starved-looking, unhealthy, except her swollen abdomen.

"You've got to take care of yourself," Sharon said, almost angrily.

"Of course." She brushed her belly, like a teenager feeling a tender pimple. "Vessel for the second generation, aren't I?"

"Nobody thinks of you that way." Sharon made herself unclench her fists. "You're not on the refugee ships anymore, Marie. Not some number lost in the shuffle, not some DNA strands recorded in a geneticist's computer. Call me short-sighted, but *you're* what I see, Marie. You. And you have a baby coming, and you and Jacob *want* that baby, and having that baby takes a lot out of you, so you'd better take care of yourself!"

Marie stepped slowly, almost reluctantly, away from the window.

"I'll help you suit up," Sharon said, knowing she wouldn't be able to manage all the tubes and clasps on her own. It wasn't that she needed strength or lacked knowledge of the procedure, Marie just didn't have the patience anymore to fit everything together. She got irritated, impatient, dispirited easily, far too easily. Sharon had called Jacob once, asked if she should have any pills or anything, but there was nothing really wrong, he said, just some stress and excitement, and maybe a little homesickness. When he had talked to Marie himself, she insisted there was nothing wrong.

Three of the iron trees still stood, the oldest and thickest, trunks still solid though streaked with rust. The rest lay in sandy piles across the yard—Sharon had directed her gardener to sweep them up, but he had been busy lately, working on the new cactus garden.

Marie looked at the trees but said nothing, as if she lacked the strength for a rebuke.

"My climate-read says the humidity's fifteen percent today," Sharon said, mostly for the sake of saying something. "Not bad. Wind's from the south, of course, but we've got the suits on in case it changes …"

"Of course," Marie said. "Wouldn't want to dry out, would we?"

Sharon led her to the iron bench. She was always leading her places, it seemed, or coaxing her to eat, or helping her suit up or bathe. No lover's touches, anymore. She felt more like an old wife helping her spouse dying of some wasting disease.

Morbid thought. She shook it off.

"I wonder what it's like on other planets," Marie said. "If they've had to change them so much. Probably wouldn't have to import hydrogen on Prometheus, I've heard it's pretty wet there anyway …"

"All sorts of places," Sharon said. "I guess it's different everywhere." She supposed it meant something, that Marie would expend the energy to wonder.

The boot of Marie's hydrosuit scuffed the sand. "Imagine," she said, "All the colonies they've set up—how many are there? Over twenty?"

"Something like that."

"And almost all of them had life of their own before we came. Life that's evolved for millions of years and then… done." She pointed at a mound of rusty sand.

"It happens," Sharon said, though of course it didn't, not in the natural order of things.

But since when did the natural order count for anything?

"Of course," Marie said. "Look at Earth."

Sharon was about to ask what she meant when the pointing finger went from the sand mound to a wiggling thing tucked in a silica bush's shadow and Marie gasped, "What's that?"

"That?" Sharon stood and crept closer, slowly, so it wouldn't run or wiggle away. "It's, um… a sand-waver, maybe."

"Maybe?" Marie followed her.

"They don't usually look like this."

The thing wiggled harder as they approached. Probably a sand-waver—that wiggling might be the weary echo of its usual graceful glide. No wonder, though, that this one wasn't more graceful. The shell covering its head, which normally made it look like a horseshoe crab formed by a turtle glued onto a tadpole (Jacob's words, Sharon remembered from some party, describing the things to some other Earth-natives attending, Marie clinging to his arm; maybe this was the party where she had met her), had sloughed off, like something melting. Wrinkled shards lay scattered across the sand, and the body they revealed was pale brown, wet-looking, and twisting in obvious pain.

"Oh ..." Marie said.

"Yeah." Sharon turned away. Time to go inside, for sure. Marie didn't need to see this—

"*Oh*," she said again. Sharon looked over her shoulder to see her kneeling, reaching out, and before she could stop her, gathering the creature into her arms.

"I'm not sure ..." The warning died in her mouth. What might happen? The sand-waver couldn't hurt Marie through the suit, and she didn't seem to be doing it any more harm.

"Sharon, can we help it? Is there anything we can do?"

"I don't know." She had never known a sand-weaver to grow back shell, though admittedly she'd never known one to lose it either, and it wasn't like anyone on Diana studied how to treat water-poisoning. She assumed that was what it was. She didn't have drying-suits or dehumidifiers or anything like that.

"Sharon, let's take him inside." Marie's eyes were wide, her words rushed; she seemed panicked.

"I can't. It's even damper in there."

"Oh. Right ..." She was biting her lip, Sharon could see through the mask. Then, "Why couldn't you have had a shield? I told you to put one up... It was your idea in the first place—it would have saved them, don't you see? It could have saved them! Why didn't you do it?"

The reasons were long, complex, and too weak to give her, Sharon knew, too weak to stand against Marie's frustrated sobs. The only thing strong enough to stand against anger was anger, so she said, "It wouldn't have done any good, anyway."

"What?"

"Look, you know it! This planet's dying. We're drowning it, making it all nice and perfect for humans to live on—killing everything that's evolved to live on it in the first place! I could save a dozen trees or a sand-waver, but what good does that do, really? Nobody else cares. Eventually I'll die, and the estate will go to somebody who doesn't give a damn, and the shields will go down, and they'll all die. So why bother?"

"Why both ..." Marie broke off, looking at the sand-waver in her arms. It had stopped wiggling. "I always thought you'd bother."

"I don't anymore. I'm sick of being the only one who cares."

"I care," Marie said. She crouched and set the sand-waver down, on the pile of rusty sand at her feet. "I've always cared. About what we're doing to this planet—about what we're doing to ourselves. About what we did to Earth. We killed it." She stepped to the bench, mechanically, and dropped into it. "And to save the human race, we split up families, we divided our DNA to give our descendents a good genetic heritage, and now we massacre ecosystems so they'll have the right sort of environment. And some people cared—we didn't want to lose our children, you didn't want to lose your planet, but... so what?"

"Yeah," Sharon said. "So what? It's the future of the human race."

"Bullshit."

She sat down beside the shaking figure in the hydrosuit. "I love you, Marie."

"Thanks."

But she wouldn't stop crying. An Earth-native habit, that; children on Diana were taught better than to waste water on tears. It was a show of respect, mainly, for the preciousness of water—nobody was really put in danger of dehydration by crying.

This, the death of a planet, was surely an occasion for tears if there ever was one.

Sharon, dry-eyed, put her arms around Marie and held her for a long time.

When she awoke, the other side of the bed was empty.

It hadn't been, the night before—Marie had been there, and though they hadn't made love in the literal sense they had held each other, kissed, spoken softly about nothing until they fell asleep.

It was good, she supposed, that Marie was out of bed so early. Usually she slept in, even until noon some days. If she had more energy, or at least the will to use it, perhaps the scene in the garden yesterday had been worth it.

Sharon rolled out of bed, dressed, hummed softly as she went downstairs. It was an old song, one she hadn't heard for a while but always remembered, a lullaby. She thought Marie might like to hear it.

Marie wasn't in the dining room as she had expected. She went to the parlor door, peered in—nothing—and was halfway to her study before she realized that Marie wouldn't have gone in there without her. Thinking she might be in the bathroom, she had decided to go into the dining room and wait when the door at the far end of the hall opened.

"Ma'am ..."

"Tom." She turned, saw his face; she ran down the hall to the foyer. "What is it?"

He pointed, vaguely, behind him. No words.

Sharon opened her closet, grabbed down a hydrosuit and fumbled it on. She was pulling the mask over her head as she ran out the door.

No native of Diana, no matter her hurry, would step outside without a suit.

The fact seemed both irrelevant and deeply vital.

She hung from the tallest tree, a blur of rose pink—the color of her nightshirt and her chapped skin. Bare feet dangled above an overturned chair. How could she not have noticed it missing from the dining room?

She hadn't worn a hydrosuit or a mask. Sharon couldn't look at her face—she knew what happened to eyes when someone died that way, and she knew what happened to eyes without a mask, they'd shown her videos in grade school.

Though Diana had been drier, then.

"Tom," she called. "Get... somebody. The police, maybe. And tell Jacob. But... we need somebody to get her down... hurry!" The branches of the remaining iron trees were still study, mostly, not rusted through or even near it, and Marie was slight, but Sharon imagined her body as an unbearable burden; at any moment she expected the branch holding her to snap.

"Yes, ma'am." She heard, faintly, the door closing behind him.

Thoughts, then, falling like drops of water.

She should have gotten the shield.

Jacob had no family on Diana now, though he had some children on Mars, Janus II, and Prometheus.

Those children would never know.

Diana was still dying, and she was back to being the only one who cared.

She had told Marie she loved her. She couldn't remember ever saying it before.

"Bullshit." She didn't know what she was saying it to; everything, perhaps. It would be nice if it was all bullshit, if none of it was worthwhile or true.

She felt liquid pooling around her chin. Her face felt wet—she realized she was crying. She pulled off her mask and stood, staring at the base of the tree, her tears drying in the arid western wind.

Easy Sweeps of Sky

Sequel to "Made Light" in *TFF* 29 (2014)

Melissa Moorer

Butterfly Fact: As with most insects (bees, fireflies, beetles), the mechanism of flight for butterflies cannot be found or explained by current aerodynamic theory.

When I got back to my tiny apartment, the window was open and the sheets were glittering, the bed unmade, which meant she'd been here and gone again. She didn't leave a written note, but this was pretty much the same thing: 'Miranda was here,' possessive form. She'd slept in my bed, used my computer, which jolted to life when I accidentally backed into my desk and hit the mouse. At least she made me coffee. It was still warm and strong. The apartment was freezing.

I closed the window but didn't lock it. Just in case. But she never returned this quickly after a visitation. Even on my birthday. She didn't leave a present either. Probably better that way.

We'd agreed to separate, to put our 'thing' on hold while we both went to college then grad school far apart. Or I thought we did. But Miranda stopped speaking to me. That's not true. She just made herself completely unavailable. New phone, new email address. Probably new twitter account I hadn't been able to find. Her old account occasionally retweeted something innocuous, but never responded to my DMs. Everything I sent her via any medium bounced or just vanished.

Which was its own message.

And so was the miserable, lonely existence I'd found myself wandering around in since. I had no idea what she was up to. Probably crime-fighting from the skies or maybe she was the villain on a crime spree. She'd always been good with the new magic—computer programming—so every time I saw some new billion dollar bank hack, I thought of Miranda bent over her laptop eating skittles, tapping ferociously, the colors on her skin getting more vivid, more lit, with her excitement.

And not just about programming.

I did not want to think about that. About Miranda and excitement.

Damn. Now I was starting to float or maybe flutter or whatever. My boots were the only thing holding me to the floor. I'd probably have to sleep in them again. And now the iridescence on the sheet was laughing. Not at me, I told myself. Not at me. Just that unreserved joy that seemed to come from everywhere when I started to be the thing that flew and heard voices in anything with light.

I closed my eyes, but the glitter and lights were still whispering just low enough so I couldn't hear what they were saying, but it was clear enough. I was a coward and I'd lost the best thing that had ever happened to me. Not lost. Thrown away. And Miranda made sure she stayed lost. I sat on the windowsill and and watched the lights of the city chatter and wink. Everything seemed flirtatious tonight. The stoplight winked sexily and I rolled my eyes.

Damn her. She knew I wouldn't be able to sleep tonight. I'd wake up bumping against the ceiling. Again. That was probably the point.

My computer hissed to life and a video began playing. It was jerky and dark, a familiar roar filling the mic, small glints and flashes of light. Then a series of winks and chirps with a familiar rhythm and shape to them. My old chrome flashlight. The one with the rounded end she said looked like a dildo. She'd never given it back and she was flying somewhere high above the city, the flashlight calling in a way that made me ache and float even with the heavy boots on.

She was reminding me of the fairy tale. She was reminding me, the grad student who spent all of her time in research, how to search. And what to search for.

I'd spent my life looking for something: my father, a career, now maybe Miranda. Because she'd found me then. I hadn't been looking. She said it was my calling or nature or something when we still talked about these things. When I almost believed all that crap about fireflies and butterflies and specialness. It's hard to believe in things the world is telling you every day aren't true.

She was going to make sure I kept looking for her for a long time. At least I knew she was close. I just had no idea how to reach her or even if I should. But the lights reminded me that I hadn't begun to really look for her. I took off my boots and opened the window.

Always Left Behind

Jack Hollis Marr

Tobias came by for me this morning. He's a strong young man and he lifts me easily, but I don't hate it the way I used to, before they left. He never makes me feel like a child. And he's good-looking too, which never hurts, though it did smart worse, before, thinking of how I must look, how he would never look at me. Tobias looks at me sometimes, I think, with that considering warmth. It makes me flustered, which an old man like me has no right being. I think about my dignity too much. The younger ones don't bother about it, not in the same way. Not with shame. They have more true dignity than the rest of us were ever allowed.

While he drives, Tobias tells me about the episode he had last night. "Angels," he says, "right out of old books, all wings and eyes." It takes me by surprise: I'd been picturing pious china figures in Victorian nightgowns, heads bowed and wings neatly folded. "Was terrified. But they was wonderful things, for as long as I could look. I thought of them old words—*be not afraid*." He always does surprise me, Tobias. There's too much of the old world left in me, expecting too little from someone like him.

Someone like him.

He helps me out of the truck and my two crutches get me into work. I call them Lefty and Righty, the way my wife called her breasts before she went off to the new world. It's not even a bitter joke. They're part of me, in their way, like her breasts were part of her. Like mine were, once, before they ended up rotting in some medical landfill; good riddance to them. I never had names for them.

My hands ache as I type. Pain's a constant, of course. No amount of looking after each other, of designing this left-behind world around us, can take that away, no more than it can take away the pain Tobias feels, the times he doesn't come, when I don't see him for days or weeks, and he comes back thin-faced and with new scars that I can see or not-see but feel. We were idealists in our own way too.

"Morning," Laverne says, coming in with tea. I wrap my aching hands around the cup. She's my age, or older, broad as a bus and half my height, and she could probably kill a man with the hands that passed me that warm mug. Two of her cats have followed her, curious; one comes to lie on my desk, in my paperwork. There are things that don't change. She goes off again quick. She doesn't do social, our

Laverne. The cat in my in-tray stays, purring low. "Scat," I tell it, "shoo," but it just blinks its slow blink and looks away. They didn't take animals to Mars, just cow-goo, pig-goo, horse-goo, all in vats. I wonder what it's like, being all alone, the only living things up there besides what they grow.

They sent messages, for a while, and then stopped. Sometimes I think maybe they all died out. Good riddance to them. It's an unworthy thought so I say a low little prayer under my breath, not for them but for myself, for all of us who can't risk thinking like that, not now. I still think it, though. We're still human, whatever they thought.

There were exceptions, of course, that they publicized broadly: the brilliant mind in the crippled body, the fat old woman who'd invented the very technology of their exodus. Those of us they took, they sterilized: no chance of reproduction, of passing on of our fatal flaws, in their dry red Eden. I'm surprised they didn't do the same to those they left behind. Perhaps they thought we'd die out anyway, slow or quick, in the ruined world they'd left us, helpless without them. Perhaps they believed we'd find each other too repugnant to mate with, or be too horrified at the idea of perpetuating our faults, our sicknesses, our fat, our twisted bones and broken minds, in another generation. Most likely they never thought about it, I suppose. They never did think about us much.

Maybe I think about them too often, up there in the sky like Tobias' angels should be, safe and far away and sending down messages of goodwill. They've got a star and all, that low red dot on the horizon some days. Shun tells me I'm counter-revolutionary, wondering about them, what they'd think of what we've made, whether they'd be surprised and think it good, or just see it as crooked and cobbled together just like us. Shun's young, though: ey don't remember what it was like before. "There's no *them*," ey say, frustrated with me, "not any more. Just *us*." Ey walk easily, are tall and straight and slim. Maybe sometimes I see em as *them*, for all I know that's wrong with em. *Wrong with*: counterrevolutionary words. There's nothing wrong with us.

But if there's no *them*, what does revolution mean? I think sometimes Shun sees me as them, for everything ey say: a familiar them ey've always known, a them safe to argue with. But I like em, though ey drive me crazy. And I get to call myself that now, whatever anyone (Shun) says. It's my word now, and I hug it tight.

It's my world now, ours; made not so much of ramps and gadgets as Tobias' real indifference as he lifts me out of bed, Laverne's practical hands wiping my arse clean when I shit myself. It's a better word than pretty was, and I shed that one a long time ago. People like Shun don't need those words, perhaps, the ones I cuddle both for comfort and to protect them: *crazy, broken, cripple, freak.* My words, my self, bridging this old world and this new with my twisted-up self. I think of it like that, my crumbling spine like the gaps in the swinging rope bridge from old films when the heroes were strong men and the bad guys were us, broken or brown, too lisping, too womanly, too strange. We'll be dead soon, my generation, and the young ones won't remember things like that, and the world they build may be amazing because they never remember those that left us behind. But sometimes, when Laverne brings me a hot drink, our eyes meet, kind and cynical at once. Yes, they don't know how good they have it, how bad it was, uphill both ways in the snow. We both look forward to dying, someday, like Tobias does all the time. I'll help him, when he asks.

Not long for me, now. I flex my hands, all bone and thick hair and hurting. They've done good work, when they can. I think of how they'll be rotting someday soon, like my long-good-riddance breasts, like Shun's lover's flesh turned on itself. *Eyesore* means what my eyes are like a lot of the time now, from squinting in the light. We that are left, made of imperfection, in a world too bright for me to see, like staring into the sun: like Tobias' angels, all blazing wings and eyes. My ears can't hear what tidings they bring, tell if we should be joyful or sore afraid. *Sore* like the ones on Shun's lover's face that Shun kisses so gently and never sees an eyesore.

Ah, it's too much for me. I flex my hand again and go back to work. My world's a small one, when I don't think these thoughts, and I like it that way. For all they call me *Father*, I don't have any great blessings to give, only small and broken ones. Like me, and I smile a bit, erase and re-write a piece of my sermon. Though they're not my gods, maybe Tobias' angels are watching over us; maybe they'll bless us, like they should, from far away. I like to think we don't need them, not any more. Bent, broken, crippled and crook'd: who needs blessings? (All of us, all of us who know and share this terrible pain.) So I'll have to do it, as best I can, with my crooked hands. Bless myself, and Tobias and Lavern and Shun and Shun's lover and all of us, the new grand-baby crying in its crib behind Laverne's office door: bless us every one.

"In general, normal medical and physiological health standards will be used. These standards are derived from evidence-based medicine, verified from clinical studies.

- The applicant must be free from any disease, any dependency on drugs, alcohol or tobacco;
- Normal range of motion and functionality in all joints;
- Visual acuity in both eyes of 100% (20/20) either uncorrected or corrected with lenses or contact lenses;
- Free from any psychiatric disorders;
- It is important to be healthy, with an age- and gender-adequate fitness level;
- Blood pressure should not exceed 140/90 measured in a sitting position;
- The standing height must be between 157 and 190 cm."

From astronaut selection qualifications for Mars One mission.[1]

---

[1] http://www.mars-one.com/faq/selection-and-preparation-of-the-astronauts/what-are-the-qualifications-to-apply

Outlaw Bodies
Seven prologues and an epilogue

Lori Selke

1. The history of science fiction begins with an outlaw body. Dr. Frankenstein fabricates a creature from spare body parts and some sort of secretive scientific process; his hubris then comes into conflict with his creation's drive for autonomy and an identity, a place in the world, a name. Meanwhile, the creature also wrestles with his own hubris and his own capacity for violence and destruction—his own body's rogue capabilities.

2. I grew up reading Chris Claremont-era X-Men comics. Mutants, too, are outlaw bodies, expressing strange powers that sometimes reshape their appearance. The X-Men have been discussed as a metaphor for puberty, for coming out as part of the LGBTQ community, even for racial difference. My favorite X-person was Storm; I probably had a crush on her, especially after she had a nervous breakdown, cut her shockingly white hair into a mohawk and started walking around in a leather jacket. My second favorite was Nightcrawler, probably because of his campy love of old swashbuckling movies and the contrast between his fearsome face and his gentle soul. Nightcrawler was secretly your queer uncle.

3. For a short time, I worked as a proofreader for a transhumanist-themed magazine. When the articles dealt with the corporeal at all, the topics were always about how to hack your body to defy aging and death. Which, if you stripped away the SF-speak and squinted, didn't make it all that different in content from women's magazines in the end.

4. The man on the bus giving me the stink-eye in the hopes that I won't sit next to him—is he trying to ward me off because I am fat? Because I am visibly gender-nonconforming? Or is there some other invisible reason? I'll never know. My body is not an outlaw body, not quite. But it is an outlier body. It always has been and it always will be.

5. Bodies exist in the tension between form and chaos. The body seems self-contained, but it is not self-sustainable. The body is a medium of exchange. Bodies also exist in the tension between self and community. Outlaw bodies are considered disordered but in fact they cannot be, or else they would not be bodies any more. Outlaw bodies follow a different order. An unsanctioned order. They problematize the

individual in context.

6. I hate being a spokesperson, especially a solo representative. It's a heavy weight that overprivileges my limited perspective on things. I prefer panels to presentations. I like dialog and I like cross-talk. Anthologies thus hold a special appeal to me. I don't have to articulate my own, often limited ideas on a subject; I can just gather the right people and let them do it for me. The best anthologies sound less like a chorus and more like medieval polyphony. There is no need to harmonize, but a pleasing pattern is created nonetheless.

7. I'm pleased that *Outlaw Bodies* was published in both book and e-book form. In a way, it neatly recapitulates the post-cyberpunk tension in SF between physical and electronic bodies and allows for a both/and that tickles my sensibilities.

Epilogue
A post-publication free association on the subject of outlaw bodies past, present and future:

Skin. Membrane. Fluid exchange. Fitbit. Black Lives Matter. The body is not an apology. Can you hack jet lag? Slut Walks. Dress codes. Refugees/migrants/citizens. Mom bod. Dad bod. Bikini bod. Trans bodies. The death penalty. Kidney failure. Liver damage. Chemical endangerment. Pneumonia. What you know about steroids is wrong. Chemotherapy. Disability justice. Hero-monsters. Zombies. Virus. Vaccines. Shingles. Toxoplasmosis. Designer drugs. Cosmetic surgery. Bariatric surgery. Pregnancy. Transvaginal ultrasounds. Repetitive stress. Human-machine interfaces. Seamless. Secondary sexual characteristics. Remote control. Control. Out of control. Microcontrol. Regulated. Deregulated. Unregulated. Decriminalized. Legalized. UX. Human error. Functionality. Smart. Structured. Connected. Disruptive. Disrupted. Signal. Noise. The surveillance state. Renewable. Sustainable. Machine empathy. Alive.

Thick on the Wet Cement

Rebecca J. Schwab

hold it for you now.
looks heavy I would like to
In your hands your face

I write them like that so when she's walking she can read them in the right order. Her face never leaves the sidewalk directly in front of her, and I use colored chalk to make them stand out from the bleak cement and tossed away gum wrappers. I saw her resting by the library like that two weeks ago, sitting on the narrow concrete retaining wall where the homeless people usually hang out. She didn't have an expression on her face as she stared at the ground and I hardly ever see her still. She's usually walking.

At first I mistook her for a man. She wears a baggy, gray ARMY shirt and black swishy track pants, her breasts loose and hanging just over her waistband. When it's hot she trades the pants for a pair of black spandex shorts. Her stomach protrudes and I wonder if it's held babies that are grown now. Her cropped dark hair is sprinkled with silver and she is always alone.

A friend of mine, Bryan, said that one day he saw her stomping on a man as he lay on the sidewalk. She didn't say anything as she drove her sneaker down on his ribs. The man was curled into a ball on his side, whining like a small frightened animal. Bryan didn't know why she was so angry.

After weeks of seeing her do laps around Morgantown, I decided to say hello. *Don't do it,* Bryan told me over the telephone, reminding me of the man on the sidewalk. But I thought someone who is always alone might like to have a conversation with someone. I usually pass her on High Street on my way to Jay's Daily Grind, the coffee shop I like, and that day, in a non-threatening yellow blouse, I thought to myself, Here I go.

I inhaled as I saw her coming and I smiled. I said *Hi.* She didn't look up and I thought maybe she didn't hear me.

So I said *Hi* the next day, pausing for a moment in front of her for emphasis, like I really meant it. Not like the people who say hi just because your eyes meet theirs in line at the grocery store.

But I had to jump out of her way, because again, she didn't look up or seem to notice I was there. I cut my knee on a fire hydrant when I did this, but though it stung and bled, I didn't say *Ouch* because I was busy staring at her as she walked away from me. The scab is shaped like a mouth.

will chatter of you.
scar from the fire hydrant it
I hope I get a

I left that the next day right by the fire hydrant. I put it in pink chalk this time like the color my brand new skin will be after the smile-shaped scab falls off. I hope she saw the words and thought of me, the girl who cared enough to get out of her way, to say hello twice without being told anything in reply.

I live in a small efficiency up by the Ramada Inn, at the end of a long dead end road. Nearby, there are nicer apartment complexes, but they're more expensive and I can't afford them. The thin man who lives across the parking lot from me likes to sit outside in a folding chair. His name is Gary. I've told him lots of times that my name is Lara, but he always calls me *Young Lady*. I say *Good morning* to him and he tells me how the weather will be and what the leaves are about to do. He told me two days ago that they're about to start falling, though I thought that was obvious, and then he described the first chapter of a novel he's writing about extraterrestrials. He's working up to a large-scale battle scene in chapter ten, but told me not to worry because the humans win. I watched his hollow chest, how it heaved up and down in thin arcs as he spoke.

Aside from Gary and the mailwoman I wave to, my apartment complex is pretty lonely. It's full of retired people who stay indoors and people who often leave town for business. It has a motel feel to it, like no one is planning on staying long and no one wants anyone else to really know why they're there. I get bored a lot. There's a window in my apartment, but the only thing to look out on is the parking lot, and in nice weather, Gary. I don't have cable. Sometimes, for something to do, I construct poems out of words I cut from the free Saturday paper. I choose interesting words like *October* and *Vascular* and put them in a red plastic colander. I shake them out onto the coffee table and read them how they fall.

A few days a week, after work, I avoid going straight home to my empty apartment. I sit in the front window of Jay's on a high stool and I count how many times the walking woman passes. One day I sat there for four hours and I counted seven times. At the coffee shop you can't just sit, so I bought four large cups of cappuccino and a raspberry scone. I left the window a few times to visit the ladies' room and I hope I didn't miss one of her laps. My friend Sheila and I used to meet for coffee on Saturdays, but since she got together with her girlfriend Janie I don't see much of her. Last month, Bryan moved two hours away for a job in marketing. Aside from them, I have a few other friends, but they all have jobs or kids or spouses. They're busy. They tell me they don't have a lot of time to hang out, and I try to understand.

The woman I watch doesn't wear any makeup. Her face is brown from the sun, which makes me think she doesn't wear sunblock, either. I wonder if she'll get skin cancer because she's outside so much. I'm concerned and tell her, because that's what friends do.

> tricky mercury.
> slowly like a mad hatter's
> The sun's damage acts

I write this poem in yellow chalk, the color of *Caution,* in front of the coffee shop very early on Saturday. I sit in the window so I can see her face as she reads it. At nine-oh-six she walks right over it and her face doesn't change at all. Her eyebrows don't raise and her mouth is still a line. I don't think she likes it. Maybe she doesn't understand it. As I sip my second cappuccino I imagine smearing a greasy line of white sunblock down the bridge of her sharp nose.

Today she's wearing a hat. It's beige with a gold and blue WVU stitched firmly onto its front. Her face is scowling but safe, shaded by the protective brim. I see the shallow crows' feet around her dark eyes and I know they won't get any deeper today. Her elfish ears are still left vulnerable, but I take the hat as a sign that she liked the poem after all, that she knows someone cares for her. I leave another one, to let her know how things could be, how we could spend our Sunday afternoons in the spring.

> Both of your eyes closed.
> I'd like to read you a book
> Under a shade tree

This is on Pleasant Street, written in green because I read in a book that green is calming. I imagine what it would be like if we were friends, if she gave me a chance. We'd run into each other on High

Street near the dry cleaner's and I'd casually ask her if I could buy her a gelato. She'd be hot from exercising and say *Yes.* She might get something in a tropical flavor, like mango or pineapple or pomegranate. I would get vanilla and maybe she'd tease me for being boring. We'd sit on a bench and watch people quietly as they went by. When she left me to go home, I'd say *I'll see you tomorrow* and she'd say *Yep,* just like that, because she'd know I was telling the truth.

I work at a car dealership by the river. We don't sell many cars, especially because gas prices are so high right now. No one is buying SUVs and half of our lot is full of them, shining in the sun as they decrease in value. I sit behind a small desk that overlooks the avenue and I watch people going by on bikes. I wave to them if they look at me.

My boss doesn't come in much because business is slow. There's no one for me to talk to, since I'm the only employee besides Veronica, who files things. She's forty-three and pregnant, and on bed rest. Her doctor said she was high-risk and she can't work. My boss said *Fine,* because that's one less person to pay, though they're arguing over whether or not she'll get paid maternity leave. Even though there's nothing to file, I miss Veronica. Without her, there's no one to have coffee with. I can never drink a whole pot by myself, so I pour the leftovers into a large fern in the front window. He seems to like it. His leaves are dark green and stretch toward the sun. I've named the fern Folger, and I address him when I say something out loud at work, like *Good morning* or *I couldn't sleep again last night.* I know Folger is only a plant, but it's better than thinking in silence all day. We don't have a TV at work and I'm not supposed to make personal phone calls, though sometimes I do sneak a call to Bryan. I haven't told him about the poems.

> I could do the same.
> but he listens politely
> Folger is quiet

This one was just a practical thought I had at work and I wrote in on Willey Street just in front of the Methodist church. I printed it in white chalk since I knew the poem was stark and unlovely. I also knew the woman wouldn't know who Folger was, but thought she might get the point anyway.

After I wrote it I wandered down Willey Street and stopped in front of St. John's Catholic Church. The evenings are getting chilly and I shivered. Since I had nowhere to be I stood still and stared up at the church's windows. I wondered if I should commit myself to this parish or any parish—I was never baptized, so my choices are wide open. I thought about that—about why I haven't ever bothered with church, and I looked to my right when I heard approaching footsteps.

It was her. She wore the track pants and a fleece jacket. I shoved my chalky fingers deep into the pockets of my windbreaker and stepped forward to let her pass. I thought I heard her mutter *Thank you,* but I couldn't be sure. The wind was picking up and the college students were beginning to swarm the streets. As I looked at her receding figure, I realized that I had expected her to walk in the other direction, that the poem would be upside down to her. I hoped she could figure out the way it was supposed to be. I almost called after her, to tell her to go the other way, but a group of four screeching girls passed in front of me and cut off my view.

I drove home. It was too cold for Gary to be out. I checked for mail but there was none. I called Bryan; he was busy. Same with Sheila. I got out my scrapbook of newspaper poems and read them out loud, but none of them meant anything to me. Lying on my fold-out couch, I looked out the window until the last bit of light was gone and I could see the silhouettes of my neighbors moving behind their window shades.

Today it's raining. My wool sweater is getting damp and I'm trying to hurry because I have to be at work in an hour and I still need to get breakfast. The blue chalk writes thick on the wet cement and my words show up bold, standing out like they're on a blackboard in a classroom. I'm trying to write fast, but the rain is coming down harder and it runs into my eyes. I blink it away, wipe my forehead with my soggy sleeve.

it's chilly today.
cup of coffee or a scone
Let me buy you a

I'm shivering by the time it's finished and my blue piece of chalk is worn down to a nub. The poem is on the corner of Spruce and Willey. I get up from my crouch and jog in the direction of Jay's, squinting to keep out the water, trying not to slip in my slick-soled ballet flats. I stop when I reach High Street. Cars are driving by, taking the corner too fast, maybe because of the weather. I punch the crosswalk button and turn around, regretting that I didn't wear my raincoat.

And that's when I see her, head down, tee shirt soaked, passing the

BB&T. I freeze for a moment when I realize she's heading into the street just as a pickup is turning onto High from Willey. Frantic, I slosh through a puddle and dash the three yards that separate us. I grab her, yell *Wait.* She whirls, fierce, looks from me to her blue-smudged shoulder, my fingers still clutching her sleeve. I don't let go because I don't want to. She narrows her eyes—brown—for the first time, I'm close enough to see what color they are. I look meaningfully into them, tell her, *Hold on, I'm your friend,* but she doesn't hear me, or maybe she doesn't trust me. She grabs my forearm so hard it hurts, pinches, her fingers like metal tongs, but for just a moment, there on the street corner, we're holding onto each other. Then she shoves me down to the wet sidewalk. I land on my right hip and it hurts so much I almost cry. I lie there, stunned, rainwater pooling in my left ear. *I was trying to save you,* I yell after her, but she keeps walking.

I'm sitting in Jay's and I was supposed to be at the dealership twenty minutes ago. I'm on my second cup of hot tea and I'm not shivering as much anymore. The rain is coming down lighter now. It's warm in here and the girl behind the counter said a batch of cranberry muffins will be ready soon. My sweater is dirty from the puddle and there's a tear in the elbow I hope I can patch. My forearm aches, and I can still feel where her fingers dug in.

She's walked by twice now and she must have seen it, the blue invitation on the sidewalk. If it hasn't washed away. If she hasn't changed her route. The second time she passed she looked at me through the window and she didn't seem angry anymore. Her chin tilted up and her damp forehead wrinkled. I'm sitting across from an empty chair and I'm waiting, thinking next time, she'll stop in. She's got to be chilly by now, too.

Innervation
(poem)

Toby MacNutt

Hir first efforts had been clumsy,
creatures of bundled nails and gobbed solder
inelegantly bumbling toward the refrigerator.
Prototypes. Now ze works in wire:
thread-thin, coiled, shining russet
like an afternoon in early autumn,
harvest-time gathered and spun
as fine as cobweb. It puts hir mouse-brown hair
to shame; ze doesn't mind.

In the womb we grow rostral-caudal, medio-lateral—
beak to tail and inside out. In the lab,
the construct grows up from its fingertips.
With jewellers' tools, its creator blunts the end
of each snipped wire to a tiny flattened head,
a delicate copper nail, a pin then set amongst its fellows
in a rounded cluster, a constellation, a thistle blossom,
its prints emerging more pointillist than whorl.
Where wire-stems meet ze plies them:
clockwise, widdershins, clockwise again,
strands building upon strands, into knuckles,
into wrists, into arms. It has no skin
and needs no bones; it stands on nerve alone.
(Save for one: its spine, a solenoid ascending,
filled with all the stubbornness of iron.)

The current flows. Urged on by its lodestone,
the copper creature bristles: each tiny filament
as lively as if goosebumped. Its head is a wire cloud,
intricate, organic, a chaos-theory temari
bright with jumping sparks. Nearby speakers whine and crackle
to its pulse, and the ancient monitor dances,
its screen a warped rainbow. The flickers fade.
The golem merely stands: all cabled limb
and delicate metallic fur, hammered pin-heads
bouncing light between. It seems to shimmer.

Ze reaches, and the speaker-hum quickens.
It sways toward hir like a vine toward the light.
It is warm to the touch—but ze feels no sting, no shock,
just a thousand-thousand tiny prickles
as animated wires meet, for the first time,
the shifting boundaries of skin.

Ephemeral Love

Melanie Rees

Deep within, something churns. A mechanical heartbeat pierces its way to the surface infringing upon the tranquillity, as the sun sinks and surrenders to the numinous night. Amphibians croak in the rich primordial swamps. A myriad of other creatures join in and impart their tunes to the exultant chorus.

In the distance, the silhouette of the mechanical down-shaft seems to be calling, almost beckoning. He stands on the precipice, loyalties divided between obligation and something that remains undefined. He needs to remain here, to dwell in her golden aura, comforted by her tender melodies and vibrant hues. But his commitments seem to overshadow everything else. The masters of the underworld trigger something deep within; an instinctive mechanism tells him that he must abide.

In ungainly fashion, he lumbers towards the shaft. An opaque tubular carriage rises to the surface and with digits of ill-designed dexterity he programs the sequence that will take him to the lower levels of the ancient hibernaculum. The carriage doors close and stars vanish one by one, as he is plunged into darkness and vertical descent. The darkness is not soothing like the visual silence of the night sky, rather an unnatural emptiness: rigid and unmoving. Over the eons he has never felt the urge to unplug, to vanish. Perhaps this is what they once called fear. He flips an internal switch and tunes out to the black commotion.

The carriage opens and reawakens him. Trudging from the hateful elevator, ancient sensor lights are triggered, illuminating the vast antechamber. Although a thick film of dust has settled and a few rodents have taken up residency, it still looks like it did all those millions of years ago.

There are four walls, each sharing a certain grandeur, a certain regality: although they pale in comparison to *her*. The plasma-infused wall surrounding the down-shaft shines with thousands of images from an age long forgotten. He counted them once, only sixty two thousand, three hundred and seven relayed over and over again: images of people smiling out from the wall at him, people holding hands, children running under sprinklers and walking with bare feet on manicured grass. On the adjacent southern and northern walls lie two huge computer screens and consoles. They span the entire length of the antechamber, powered indirectly through the solar rays captured above. Data flickers across their black surface intermittently. At the other end of the antechamber, the hibernaculum entrance dwindles in the distance.

The tinny voice of the computer echoes within the empty auditorium monotonously, *"De-stasis thawing will commence in two hours. Please accept or reject re-colonization status. De-atrophying process will commence in seventy-four hours. Please accept or reject re-colonization status… De-stasis thawing will commence in two hours …"* It continues its message repeatedly.

The whirring of the hibernaculum's de-thawing sequence starts up again, drowning out the computer's tinkling and his own thoughts.

Sluggishly he wanders across to the computer terminal and mulls over the readings. Climatic trends scroll across the screen in iridescent green lettering.

"Atmospheric methane: 1600 parts per billion. Nitrous oxide: 280 parts per billion. Carbon dioxide: 290 parts per million. Re-colonisation status: 92.3% optimisation."

Why the re-colonisation percentage is below one hundred puzzles him. Perhaps they are waiting for trees bejewelled with gold leaves.

The whirring intensifies as the second stage recolonisation process kicks into gear. He can just make out the caskets of the hibernaculum, stacked in high, tiered columns, like a tomb. Above the entrance is a golden plaque engraved with the words "Buds for the Valley of New Eden." Soon these so-called buds will blossom across fields and hillsides. Their pollen will blow in the wind to the atmosphere and wash downstream to the oceans. Everywhere will be a mass of bipedal flowers and their pollen.

Masses of them once stood in this cryostat auditorium listening and waiting. They said he would need to remember the 'love' humanity once shared and reaffirm belief in his duties.

Like all of history, he remembers it vividly, although he is still not sure that he understands.

The speaker sits next to him, adorned in full suit and tie, shielded from the scalding heat outside by the antechamber.

In an opulent voice, the suited man commands attention. "Do not fear, my fellow citizens, for our society will return. Yes, we will sleep, but we will re-awake. This fiery planet will cool, gases will dissipate, soils will become enriched, resources will become plentiful and…" The suited man's voice increases another 1.23 decibels as he raises his hands and looks up at the ceiling. "And the rain... the *rain,* my friends, will fall like it once did."

Looking up at the featureless ceiling quizzically, he searches his databanks for information on rain and retrieves images of small children in oversized gumboots splashing in muddy puddles and gastropods leaving silvery trails in wet lawns.

"And watching over us will be the Guardian, the newest R65 designed to be capable of withstanding the Venusian-like climate, which our world is spiralling towards. He will ensure de-stasis occurs when our world is perfect again. He will endure and hence we will endure. And our economy and society will blossom like the fields of wild flowers that once graced our landscape."

The auditorium fills with rapture.

The suited man's voice mellows and he reels off instructions. "If everyone would like to make their way to the hibernaculum with your lottery ticket ready, the stewards will usher you to your respective chambers."

Flanked by large men and a stately woman the suited man is ushered to his resting spot. A young woman half his age and with large belly hastens forward crying desperately.

Black suited men race forward. "You don't even have a pass, miss, please step back." They usher her away as she cries and clutches her stomach.

Slowly the crowds start filtering across the floor. Many are finely dressed with keepsakes and trinkets strung about their necks. Some are turned away from the chamber despite cries of consternation. People scramble impatiently creating a bottleneck at the entrance to the hibernaculum. A scuffle breaks out. Several brutish men in camouflaged trousers head towards the commotion. Shots ring out. The antagonist falls listlessly to the ground with a thud. Only a few young faces bother to turn around.

The commotion slowly dies down and the 'future blooms', as the suited man calls them, close up in their stasis capsules like petals closing as the sun retreats from the sky.

The auditorium becomes cold. Lifeless. Centuries pass. The computer hums monotonously. There are no other sounds.

The carriage of the up-shaft takes him to the world above. He shambles sluggishly across the cracked clay pans to a nearby rock and awkwardly lowers himself into a sitting position. Topsoil blows into the air with gusty winds. The dusty haze picks up the rays of the scorching sun. The sky glows orange behind silhouetted buildings. He watches as the buildings crumple to the ground over hundreds of years.

Millennia pass. A sound chimes throughout his head, like something hitting metal. He looks up to the scorching sky and droplets of liquid splatter upon his outstretched hand. The water trickles at first and then the skies open unforgivingly. In between the clacked clay pans, a monocotyledon germinates. A tiny leaf blade emerges, twisting and turning, capturing the sun. Several more emerge. A fleshy homogeneous green carpet spreads across the clay pan. Slowly other green gems sprout amongst the carpet. They become woody and grow tall. Far taller than him. Always reaching for the sun.

Millennia pass. The rock he sits on erodes with wind and rain. It turns to dust. He gets up and wanders across the valley. More rain falls and a pool forms downhill.

Millions of years pass. Tiny crustaceans jump and pirouette in the thin film of water. The pool grows and covers the entire valley floor. After an age undefined, it teems with life. Fish come to visit him at the lakes edge. He calls one of them Freddie. Small Diptera with delicate wings and slender legs tread lightly on the water. Freddie snaps at one with his elongated body and it sends ripples across the lake before he dives back down below. Freddie introduces him to his children, and his children's children's children. One of them has little growths on his flanks. The lake starts to become overcrowded. A great, great descendent of Freddie walks up the banks to meet him. Sedges and rushes grow, fringing the lake edge, sheltering her inhabitants as they sing to him at night. He sings back to her a reassuring lullaby. Who the lullaby is intended to reassure he is unsure. She seems to reassure him, with her light and dark, her music and tranquillity, her majestic curves and her tiny creatures.

He longs to see her again; he yearns for her tender breath and exposed soul.

"De-stasis thawing will commence in thirty minutes. Please accept or

reject re-colonization optimisation status."

The mechanical intrusion whirrs into his thoughts, pierces his circuits. Addle-pated he looks again at the giant screen that towers forebodingly above him. He cannot argue with the figures, everything is indeed perfect. Long-term climatic conditions are stable, resources have renewed, and there are promising signs of life with fish, amphibians and birds flourishing again.

He dubiously mutters to himself, "After all this time in stasis everything is indeed perfect."

He emerges from the elevator. She is there to greet him. Her rich blue veins slink down into the hills. Two birds perform a pas des deux above the river as something scampers through the undergrowth. Her morning dew glistens with the clear sunlight as if a million shards of mirrored glass have been strewn across the valley. Unparalleled beauty. Perhaps this is what they once called love? No, this feeling is not a fleeting thing; it has grown over the ages. They could not possibly have a word to describe the way he feels for her.

The churning and whirring has ceased.

"So what do you think? Should I give them another million years?" he asks the sun-kissed hills and river.

She whispers back with an earthly sigh, shrouding him in a misty blanket.

"Okay, you are right, two million would be better," he replies, and awkwardly makes his way to the horizon and beyond the valley of New Eden.

Contributors

Kathryn Allan is an Independent Scholar of science fiction and disability studies. She is co-editor (with Djibril al-Ayad) of *Accessing the Future* (2015), editor of *Disability in Science Fiction: Representations of Technology as Cure* (2013), and the inaugural Le Guin Feminist Science Fiction Fellow. Her most recent work appears in *Letters to Tiptree* and *Techno-Orientalism: Imagining Asia in Speculative Fiction, History, and Media*.

Therese Arkenberg is a freelance copyeditor and writer in Wisconsin, where she loves long walks along the Ice Age trail but can't help noticing the winters are getting briefer and warmer (Polar Vortexes aside). Her short fiction has recently appeared in *Analog* and *Beneath Ceaseless Skies*.

Djibril al-Ayad is the *nom de guerre* of a historian, futurist, writer, editor of *The Future Fire*, magazine of social-political speculative fiction, and co-editor of five anthologies. His interests span science, religion and magic; education and public engagement; diversity, inclusivity and political awareness in the arts.

Redfern Jon Barrett is a writer and polyamory rights campaigner armed with a doctorate in literature. Author of *The Giddy Death of the Gays & the Strange Demise of Straights* and the upcoming *Forget Yourself* (Lethe Press, 2016), he currently lives in Berlin with his two partners.

James Bennett is a British writer of fantasy and horror. His short stories have appeared internationally, a recent one "Broken Bridges" earning him a mention in *Starburst Magazine*. James lives in windy west Wales where he is hard at work on a fantasy series, the first volume of which comes out from Orbit Books in autumn 2016. Feel free to follow him on Twitter: @wytcheboy.

Jessica E. Birch is a fiction writer and an academic. Publications include stories in *Triangulation: End of Time* and *Andromeda Spaceways*, as well as chapters in *Gothic and Racism* and *Race and the Vampire Narrative*. Ketchup is her favorite condiment and she abhors small talk.

Bruce Boston is the author of more than fifty books and chapbooks. His writing has received the Bram Stoker Award, the Asimov's Readers Award, a Pushcart Prize, and the Rhysling and Grandmaster Awards of the Science Fiction Poetry Association. His latest collection, *Resonance Dark and Light*, is available from most online booksellers. bruceboston.com.

Jennifer Marie Brissett is British-Jamaican American and her former professions include bookstore owner and web developer. Her debut novel *Elysium* (Aqueduct Press) won the 2014 Philip K. Dick Award Special Citation and was shortlisted for the Locus and Tiptree Awards. She lives in NYC.

Rebecca Buchanan is the editor of the Pagan literary zine, *Eternal Haunted Summer*. She has been published in *Bards and Sages Quarterly*, *Cliterature*, *Hex Magazine*, *Luna Station Quarterly*, *New Realm* and *The Future Fire*, among other venues. When she is not writing, she is thinking about writing. She has decided that she wants to reincarnate as a library cat.

Neil Carstairs lives in Worcester, England, with his wife, two children and dog. He writes as the mood (and very occasionally the inspiration) takes him. His work has appeared on the web and in print and links can be found at neilcarstairs.blogspot.com.

Born in Singapore but a global citizen, **Joyce Chng** writes mainly science fiction (SFF) and YA fiction. She likes steampunk and tales of transformation/transfiguration. Her fiction has appeared in *The Apex Book of World SF* II, *Cranky Ladies of History*, *Accessing The Future* and *We See A Different Frontier*. Her urban fantasy set in Singapore is contracted under Fox Spirit Books. She can be found at A Wolf's Tale (awolfstale.wordpress.com). She tweets too: @jolantru.

Mark Harding lives in Edinburgh and has been published online and in print. He sporadically blogs on contravatar.wordpress.com. His current projects are a short story collection called 'Love among the Cyborgs,' a Many Worlds conspiracy thriller (with an appropriate multiplicity of titles), and hastening his second childhood.

C.A. Hawksmoor has a particular love of the darkness and the wilds. They write about sinister megacorporations, post-civilisation, Romantic retrofuturism, people who live in the margins, and the injuries to the broken parts of the world that are too painful to look at directly. You can find them at cahawksmoor.com.

Margo-Lea Hurwicz is an Anthropology and Gerontology professor who has loved science fiction and fantasy since the day long ago that she found, and devoured, a stack of *Analog*, *Galaxy*, and *Fantasy & Science Fiction* magazines hidden at the back of her father's closet.

Serge K. Keller (@citizenk) wrangles sentences as a journalist by day and pushes electrons around as a webmaster by night. Sometimes, it's the other way round. He's a keen reader and a *tsundoku* black belt. A former zookeeper, he also is a staunch, bearded Darwin groupie. He fondly remembers a time when it was still hip to be called a cybernaut.

Jocelyn Koehler writes speculative fiction, mystery, and other less definable stuff. Besides writing, tea and cheese sandwiches are her particular interests. Also NBA, because basketball. See what she's working on at Patreon (patreon.com/JocelynKoehler) or at her website (teamblood.org).

Alison Littlewood is the author of *A Cold Season* and its recent sequel, *A Cold Silence*, from Jo Fletcher Books. Her short stories have been picked for several horror, fantasy and crime Best Of anthologies, and won the 2014 Shirley Jackson Award for Short Fiction. Visit her at alisonlittlewood.co.uk.

Toby MacNutt lives and teaches in the state of Vermont. Hir short fiction and poetry has been published by or is forthcoming from *Through the Gate*, *inkscrawl*, and *Capricious Magazine*. When not writing, ze works in textiles and dance. You can find out more at tobymacnutt.com or say hello to @tylluan on Twitter.

Jack Hollis Marr (also published as Jack H. Marr) writes speculative fiction and poetry for adults and teens. His work often tackles issues of gender, sexuality and disability, interlaced with mythic and folkloric themes and rural life past and present.

Cécile Matthey, illustrator, photo librarian and eclectic reader, is forever attracted by imaginary worlds and strange universes of all kinds. She has illustrated stories for *TFF* since 2006 (see also: cecilematthey.ch for more), and more recently joined the reading team. She looks forward to the next memory of a possible future.

Melissa Moorer's work has been short-listed for a few awards (Glimmer Train, Pushcart, storySouth Million Writers) and published in luminous journals (*LCRW*, *Hot Metal Bridge*, *FLAPPERHOUSE*, *The Future Fire*) and *Heiresses of Russ*. She was Assistant Editor at *The Butter* where she wrote This Writer's On Fire.

Julie Novakova (julienovakova.com) is a Czech author of science fiction and detective stories. She has published short fiction in *Clarkesworld*, *Perihelion SF* and other magazines. Her work published in Czech includes seven novels, an anthology and more than thirty stories. She also translates, writes nonfiction and is a regular contributor to the Czech SF magazine *XB-1*.

Sara Puls spends most of her time lawyering, researching, writing, and editing. Her dreams frequently involve strange mash-ups of typography, fairy creatures, courtrooms, and blood. Sara's stories have been published in *Daily Science Fiction*, *GigaNotoSaurus*, *Penumbra*, several anthologies, and elsewhere. On Twitter she is @sarapuls.

Melanie Rees is an environmental consultant whose job involves working with soil and plants. When she isn't gallivanting in the mud or stuck up a tree she writes speculative fiction. Her stories and poems have appeared in markets such as *Apex*, *Cosmos* and *Penumbra*. More information on her publications can be found at flexirees.wordpress.com and on Twitter @FlexiRees.

Brett Savory is the co-publisher of the World Fantasy Award-winning and British Fantasy Award-winning ChiZine Publications, has had over 50 short stories published, and has written two novels. He recently finished his third novel, *Running Beneath the Skin*, and lives in Toronto with his wife, writer/editor/publisher Sandra Kasturi.

Rebecca J. Schwab is serves as acquisitions editor for Leapfrog Press, freelances for *Buffalo Spree*, and reports for the *OBSERVER* in Dunkirk, NY. Her work has been published in *Brevity*, *Slipstream*, *Allegro Poetry Magazine*, and elsewhere.

Lori Selke is the author of *The XY Conspiracy* (Aqueduct Press, 2013) and the co-editor of *Outlaw Bodies* (Futurefire.net Publishing, 2012). She lives in Oakland, California. Find out more at loriselke.com.

Su J. Sokol is is an activist and a writer of interstitial fiction. Her short stories have been published in *The Future Fire* and *Spark: A Creative Anthology*. Su's debut novel, *Cycling to Asylum* was long-listed for the 2015 Sunburst Award for Excellence in Canadian Literature of the Fantastic. A legal services lawyer from New York City, Su immigrated to Montréal in 2004.

Benjanun Sriduangkaew writes love letters to strange cities, beautiful bugs, and the future. Her work has appeared in *Tor.com*, *Beneath Ceaseless Skies*, *Clarkesworld*, and year's bests. She has been shortlisted for the Campbell Award for Best New Writer and her debut novella *Scale-Bright* has been nominated for the British SF Association Award.

Valeria Vitale is a researcher in nonexistent worlds and disappeared cities. When she's not busy writing and reading, you may find her staring at ancient objects in museums or modelling buildings in 3D. She is the co-editor of *Fae Visions of the Mediterranean* (2016). She enjoys stories so much that she is considering giving up reality altogether. Valeria likes ghosts, vampires and old mythologies. And crocodiles.

Stanislaw Lem wrote enough fake reviews to publish two collections of them. **Jo Walton** used to wonder how anybody could do this. She has also written twelve novels, three poetry collections and a book of non-fiction SF conversation, and won a whole bunch of awards, including the Hugo, Nebula and World Fantasy. She comes from Wales but lives in Montreal where the food and books are much better. She plans to live to be ninety-nine and write a book every year.